Courting Love

BOOKS BY JODIE WOLFE

TWINS & NEEDLES SERIES
Hearts Tightly Knit
Love in the Seams

BURRTON SPRINGS BRIDES SERIES
Taming Julia
Protecting Annie
Wooing Gertrude
Convincing Lou

TIME TO COME HOME SERIES
Abigail's Pursuit
Hannah's Quest
Sarah's Search
(coming Spring 2026)

HISTORICAL NOVELS
To Claim Her Heart
Courting Love: Three-in-One-Collection

Courting Love

Jodie Wolfe

WOLFE TRACKS PUBLISHING

CONTENTS

Courting Love

© 2025 by Jodie Wolfe

An Angel for the Cowboy © 2017, 2025 by Jodie Wolfe
Picking a Bride for Paul © 2017, 2025 by Jodie Wolfe
Wooing the Cook © 2025 by Jodie Wolfe

1ˢᵗ Edition
Print ISBN: 979-8-9989083-2-3
Ebook ISBN: 979-8-9989083-1-6
Library of Congress Control Number: 2025923329
Subjects: Christian Fiction Collection. | Romance Fiction. | Historical Fiction.

Cover and interior design by David Wolfe
Cover and interior images from Deposit Photos, iStock, and Pixabay

Published by Wolfe Tracks Publishing (2025)
Printed in the United States of America (Shippensburg, PA)
Scripture quotations are from the King James Version of the Bible.

My first praise must go to my Lord and Savior,
who daily provides hope in my life.
He's the anchor in the storms I face.

To my dear husband, David.
Every hero I create is loosely based on you.
Thank you for your constant love and support.

To Jenny and Joy. Thank you for your expertise on this
project.

A special shout-out to my brother, Kevin.
Thanks for your support through the years.

To God be the glory.

AN ANGEL FOR THE COWBOY

He that covereth his sins shall not prosper: but whoso confesseth and forsaketh them shall have mercy.

Proverbs 28:13 (KJV)

WANTED: A man of faith and means, willing to enter a marriage of convenience by April 14th. Must be a fine and upstanding citizen. No cowboys or drifters need apply. All inquiries should be sent to: E. Love in care of *Yoder Grove Gazette*, Yoder Grove, Kansas.

CHAPTER ONE

February 14, 1876,
Yoder Grove, Kansas

The staccato beating of her heart reverberated in Esther Love's ears as she read her announcement in the local newspaper. Two months to save her home and sisters. Would the Lord see fit to provide a man in time? She refused to contemplate what she'd do if no one answered her advertisement.

Her middle sister entered the tiny kitchen of the home they'd lived in all their lives. Essie snapped the weekly periodical closed and shoved it under a book.

The house hadn't been the same since Pa had died six months prior. Ma had passed almost two decades earlier when Essie's youngest sister was a babe.

A year ago, all had been right in the world, and she'd had a bright future ahead of her—a wedding to plan—but then that no-account banker had reneged on his promise.

"Essie."

Her sister's interruption was a welcome diversion from Essie's dismal thoughts.

Kitty stood with her hands planted on her slim hips. "Essie, you aren't listening to me. Why haven't you changed yet? You can't wear that to go to the sweetheart dance."

Essie glanced down at her rumpled dress and ink-stained fingers. She shoved a ringlet behind her ear. "I'm not going."

The same men who attended all the town festivities would be at the dance. None of them were suitable to come to her rescue or would consider taking on the restrictions she required. Especially since her lame-brained ex-fiancé had blabbed all over town about her being a dime novelist, an unemployed one, at that. So much for keeping it a secret.

"Runnin' from folks won't solve your problem." Teddy, her youngest sister, shoved the tails of Pa's shirt into her dungarees. Ma would've never allowed them to wear such garb, but she'd not seen fit to live long enough to take Teddy in hand. No matter how hard Essie tried, the girl refused to be tamed.

Essie stared at her eighteen-year-old sister. Teddy was at the age where she should think about finding a beau and settling down to run her own household instead of spending her time outdoors taking care of the farm. Her long, thick braid slapped her waist as she leaned against the dry sink.

Teddy speared her with a look. "Just 'cause that pesky insect went back on his word, don't mean you shouldn't try to snag some other fella's attention."

Essie refrained from rolling her eyes at her sister's poor grammar.

Kitty's brows waggled. "She's right, you know."

She snorted, glaring at her sisters. "I have no desire to go tonight and be the object of everyone's pity."

Kitty sidled up beside her and wrapped an arm around Essie's waist. "If you don't go, everyone will think you're a coward, and nothing could be further from the truth. Besides, you haven't been out of the house in weeks. We're concerned about you."

Actually, she'd slipped away a week ago to run to the newspaper office before they'd closed so she could sign up for the advertisement in today's paper, the one she hoped her sisters didn't read. Perhaps she should've disguised her name. "I've been out of the house." Too late. She wished she could retract the words as soon as they spewed from her lips. Essie hefted a sigh.

Teddy's eyebrows rose on her broad forehead, the same broad forehead they had each inherited from their pa. "When did you set foot outside of the house? You've been flailin' like a peacock in a mud pile ever since that two-bit nuisance broke off your engagement. In fact, you've been mighty tight-lipped since that day." Her sister's blue eyes narrowed. "You never told us what the bank manager wanted to meet with you about, either."

"Are you going along to the dance, Teddy?" Essie prayed the question distracted her sister. "I'll go if you will."

"Oh yes, please. It won't be any fun if you don't both attend." Kitty smiled as she reached for Essie's and Teddy's hands.

Teddy continued to stare at Essie for a moment before responding. "If it'll get Essie out of the house, I'll come along."

Essie sneaked a peek at her youngest sister. More than likely, the subject change hadn't fooled Teddy. She'd lay in wait like a flea on a hound dog, scheming for the opportune time to attack and bite. Maybe an evening away would distract Teddy from thinking about it. Then again, the chances of that were as rare as God dropping an interested man on her doorstep who would solve all her problems.

Fire blazed a trail through Jud Steele's leg as the acrid scent of blood filled his nostrils. Until now he'd avoided coming face to face with the bounty hunter, but not the fella's bullet. What decent man shot before asking questions?

The oozing wound had already soaked through Jud's dungarees. He didn't need the light of day to see what he already knew—if he didn't get help before long, he'd be a goner.

Jud bit back a groan. He wouldn't be in such a mess if it weren't for his inept cousin. *I don't know what You're trying to do here, Lord. I'm none too happy about the predicament You put me in. Nothing personal, but I hope You don't have me seeing Your pearly gates anytime soon.*

Sweat rolled down his face, and his stomach pitched. He gripped the reins tighter. "C'mon, Buster, we need to find help and somewhere that I can lie low for a while. At least until I can get those varmints off my tail."

Buster nickered and tossed his head.

A good horse was all a man needed. That, and maybe a juicy steak every once in a while. Yes siree. A horse, bed, and food. Women were a nuisance. Something he'd never cared to get himself tangled up with. Jud never planned on courting one. Ever. Apparently, his injury had addled his brain to make him even consider having a female in his life. He shoved the thoughts aside as pain seared through his leg as his horse stumbled.

If only he could find a house on the outskirts of town that would help a fella out without involving the authorities.

A minute later, a shimmer of light shone across the darkened landscape. Snow crunched beneath Buster's hooves, and Jud flipped up his collar when the wind whistled across the frigid prairie. He shivered despite the perspiration dotting his exposed skin. Or perhaps because of it.

He pulled Buster to a halt and dismounted on his good leg. When he placed weight on both feet, his injured leg buckled beneath him. He grunted and belly-crawled to the door, his breaths coming in short, choppy bursts. Jud finally reached the door, pounding on it. "Hey there, I need some help."

Silence. Not a sound came from inside the house. Jud ground his teeth and hammered against the door again.

Dark spots romped across his vision. He struggled to stay conscious, but blackness closed in.

Jud awoke sometime later to Buster nuzzling his forehead and the reins dangling beside his shoulder. His body felt as if a stampede of angry bulls had trampled it.

Give me strength, Lord. He grasped for the reins, his fingers grazed across the leather straps, missing them the first time. On the second try, he connected with them. He curled his hands around the lifeline between him and Buster. "Back, boy."

Buster shifted a step backward and then another. With the help of his horse, Jud struggled to get on his good knee. The landscape shifted and swirled. He closed his eyes against the spinning, praying the world would stop tipping.

Swallowing the bile lining his throat, Jud's limbs shook as he stood beside his horse, sweat coating his brow. Taking a deep breath, he somehow got on his horse. He wasn't sure how, and it took every ounce of energy to stay seated on Buster once he was there. Pain shot through him with each step the horse took.

Moonlight glimmered off the newly fallen snow. At any other time, he would've enjoyed the beauty around him. Instead, he hunched deeper into his coat, shivers quaking his body like a leaf trying to cling to a branch in a whirlwind. Jud's thoughts fuzzed and blurred. Pain throbbed with each beating of his heart as his lifeblood seeped down his leg.

He had to hold on. Find help.

Buster stumbled, pitching Jud across his horse's head. His body flew, weightless for a split second before crashing to the ground. The impact sucked away his breath as he rolled down some sort of embankment. Briars scratched at his cheeks and forehead, ripping flesh as he rolled over and over until his body thudded against something solid. He stopped with a yelp.

His thoughts clouded as he saw a woman peering down at him. Then he saw another one. He blinked, but they hadn't budged. A third came to join the other two. *Dear God, let them be a dream.*

A nightmare, more like it. The last thing he needed was to get tangled up with a gaggle of hens. He'd rather enter the pearly gates than have to be beholden to a bunch of women.

CHAPTER TWO

"What are we going to do with him?" Essie stared at the man who lay close to their doorstep. She never should've attended that ridiculous dance. But one thing was certain. The Good Lord answered her prayer. He'd brought her a man—so long as the fellow wasn't a cowboy. It'd be nice if he were at least conscious so she could find out.

"He's hurt bad. We need to take him inside and stop the bleedin', or he'll be dead." Teddy shoved the door open. "Kitty and I'll carry his legs. Step over his head there, Essie, and then get under his arms and support his upper body."

The three grunted as they lifted the man. A mixture of musk, sweat, and the pungent scent of blood filled Essie's nostrils. She shuddered at the odor. They'd been able to move him about ten steps into the kitchen before their arms gave out.

The man's brown eyes fluttered open and then closed again. Scratches marred his pale cheeks and forehead, and blood trickled from two nasty cuts under his eyes. His skin had already bruised.

Teddy stooped down and examined the man's leg. She removed Pa's belt from her waist, slipped it above the wound, and tightened the leather strap.

A gasp escaped the man's blue lips before he lost consciousness again.

"Kitty, start heatin' some water and then light all the lamps." Teddy put pressure on the man's wound. Blood seeped between her fingers. "Essie, fetch a clean towel."

"We can't possibly consider having him stay in the house with us." Essie wrung her hands. "It isn't suitable."

"Well, he can't rightly stay in the barn when it's this cold. Besides, nobody ever comes out to visit us anyway, so who'll know?" Teddy didn't glance up, but motioned with her head. "You two get movin.'"

Essie scurried to get a clean towel, while Kitty lit a lantern and then the stove.

With the advertisement Essie had posted in the paper, it was likely men would soon be visiting. Hopefully, fellows interested in her terms. She corralled her thoughts as she handed a cloth to her youngest sister and then helped Kitty retrieve the remaining lanterns.

In Pa's room, Essie gathered the small crate of supplies they'd used whenever one of them had an injury. She held the box in one arm and snagged the lamp with the other. Back in the kitchen, she deposited the items on the table. "Do you think one of us should ride over to Doc Master's place?"

Kitty shook her head. "Won't do any good. At the dance, his ma said he'd be in Iowa for a couple of weeks. Seems his sister has a malady the docs can't figure out, and she asked her brother to come to see what he could do. We need to get the bullet out of this fella, or we'll lose him."

"B-bullet? Did you say, bullet?" Essie nearly dropped the glowing match. Her fingers shook as she lifted the glass chimney and lit the wick before lowering it back into place. "Do you think he's some sort of criminal?" So much for a man to solve all her problems.

"I reckon right now it don't matter who he is. We can get that all straightened out later, but for now, we have to keep him alive. Essie, come press on his leg while I get things ready." Teddy barked additional commands to Kitty, which sent her scurrying through the house, retrieving items.

Essie kneeled beside her sister and the stranger.

"I'm going to move my hands, and you'll need to bear down hard." Teddy shifted to make more room for her.

When Essie caught sight of her sister's bloodied hands, Essie's stomach lurched and she gulped.

"Come on, there's no time to be squeamish. I need you." Teddy grabbed Essie's hand and placed it on top of hers. "Ready? In two. One. Two."

Essie applied pressure to the wounded man's leg. His eyes flickered open, and he stared at her. Pain flashed across his cheeks, and she loosened the pressure a smidge.

"Don't let up." Teddy's words jolted Essie back to the task at hand.

A hiss escaped his bruised lips as she put more weight on the wound, trying to ignore the sticky blood oozing between her fingers.

"Is he going to die?" Kitty stood off to the side. Her cheeks paled, and she bit her lip as tears rolled down her cheeks.

"Nobody's dyin' if I can help it." Teddy tugged out a pocketknife and slit the fabric, exposing the man's leg. "Kitty, bring me the alcohol."

Ma had hated having the stuff in the house, but Pa had insisted on it for such purposes.

Essie glanced back down to find the man's lips moving. She bent closer to try to catch a word or two.

His breath puffed against her cheek. "Are you an angel?"

Long brown hair fell in ringlets around the beauty's waist. The scent of flowers tickled Jud's nostrils. At the top of the white filmy high-necked part of her dress lay a black satin ribbon with a silver cross hanging from it. The Good Lord must've seen fit to call Jud home. Except if the angel was with him at the pearly gates, why did he feel such pain? And weren't angels in the Good Book men?

He blinked, but the vision didn't disappear. A frown puckered her forehead. Had he said something wrong? Surely the Lord wouldn't have such a fine creature to welcome folks into hell. Besides, he'd made peace with God years ago, and knew where he'd be heading when he died. So why was she preventing him from getting into heaven?

His sluggish brain rolled the thought back and forth across his mind as he noted her slim wrists, above the hands that were putting pressure on his leg. That's where the cattle brand burned like a blaze. "Stop. Please."

She shook her head as moisture lit the corners of her eyes. "I can't."

"Lemme go. I'm ready." If he had an ounce of energy, he'd shove her hands aside, but he couldn't even wiggle a finger.

"I'm sorry." The moisture pooled and then overflowed down her cheeks like a tiny waterfall.

"Good, you're awake." Another angel appeared beside the beauty. This gal was dressed like a fella, though. "Here, I'm going to lift your head, so you can drink some of this."

His nose wrinkled at the smell, and he frowned. Alcohol. He never touched the foul stuff. Was it some sort of test? Jud pressed his lips tight together. The evil one couldn't make him drink it.

"We have to get the bullet out, and it's going to hurt something fierce, so you'd better drink some of it." The rough one yanked his head up and pried his lips open. His fool body refused to obey him as she poured fire down his throat. He choked, sputtered, and tried to spit it out, but the woman clamped his lips shut and rubbed his throat. The liquid inferno blazed down to his gut.

Another head loomed beside him, this one fair-haired compared to the other two. "Don't die, mister. The world still needs you."

Jud wasn't sure when the world had ever had need of him. He studied the first angel, whose lips trembled as she smiled. He'd never seen something so dazzling in all his life. If he had someone like that to live for, maybe he'd choose to settle down one day.

"Kitty, find a stick or something for him to chomp on, and put a blanket under his head."

The blonde scampered out of his sight, but soon came back with a rush of cold air surrounding her.

He shivered as she placed a wooden spoon handle in his mouth. What kind of place had he found himself in? He'd never thought much about heaven, but he'd expected things to be better than this. Wasn't there a verse in Scripture that talked about no more tears and pain?

Jud about hit the ceiling when the rough one poured alcohol on his leg. The spoon dropped from his teeth.

Tears continued to stream down the first angel's cheeks. Blood covered her hands and pooled on the floor.

The evil one poked a finger in his wound, and it took everything in him not to scream.

The fair one had tears on her face as well. She edged the handle closer, and he clamped onto it again.

"Please hurry. You're hurting him, Teddy." His angel stared at her bloody hands, appearing to sway, but he couldn't say for sure since his vision kept blurring.

The evil one grunted. "I'm not tryin' to. The bullet's just out of reach."

Bullet? Why would there be bullets in heaven?

"I can't bear to watch anymore." The fair one disappeared from his sight.

His angel stayed with him, whispering encouraging words. He couldn't catch all of them, but at least she was on his side. She wouldn't do anything to injure him.

Merciful day, maybe his sweet angel could stop the evil one from hurting him so. He winced.

The rough one dug into his leg as if searching for a buried bone. "There! Got it." Something hard thudded against a pan as the wicked one stared at him. "Pour the alcohol onto the wound again, Essie."

"I'm so sorry." His angel's hand shook as she raised the bottle over his wound.

"Just do it, Essie. I need to sew him up quick-like. The longer we wait, the more we risk infection settin' in."

Liquid spilled from the bottle, and the divine messenger turned her back to him. Why had she betrayed him, too? He cried for them to stop and tried to move away from the embers blazing up his leg, but his body refused to cooperate. When he couldn't handle the pain any longer, black nothingness enveloped him like a warm blanket.

Chapter Three

I s he dead?" Essie stood in the doorway to Pa's room, afraid to step across the threshold in case her words were true. Kitty hovered at her elbow.

Teddy lifted the blanket and checked the wound. "You two are such ninnies." She shook her head, her long braid slapping against her waist.

Essie moved past Kitty and joined Teddy beside the bed once the covers were back in place. The man lay sprawled on Pa's bed. It had taken several tries to get the stranger's deadweight into the room. Morning light splashed across the man's bruised face.

She winced, imagining his pain, and couldn't resist reaching out and lightly running a finger down his cheek. Heat blazed beneath her fingertips. "He feels too warm."

Teddy placed her hand on his forehead. "Not a good sign. He must be fightin' some sort of infection the way his fever is ragin'. There's no way we can move him to the barn when he's like this. He'll have to stay in the house."

"But—"

A knock thudded against the outside door.

"I'll get it." Kitty's skirt swirled as she left the doorway and headed to the kitchen. She returned a few seconds later. "It's a strange fella, and he's asking for you, Essie."

Essie's hands flew to her hair, smoothing it into place. She ran her suddenly damp hands along the sides of her dress as her middle sister followed her. "Kitty, m-maybe it's best if you stay here and help Teddy." Her pulse skittered as she waited for either of her sisters to respond.

Teddy hiked an eyebrow but didn't say anything.

Essie inhaled a deep breath as she entered their small kitchen.

A short, balding man stood with hat in hand. A bushy mustache totally covered his upper lip, and his beady eyes watched her like a cat ready to pounce on its prey.

She bit back a shudder. "May I help you?"

"Are you E. Love?" He shifted closer and dropped to one knee. "If you are, then it would be an honor to have you as my wife."

Her heart thudded in her chest like a herd of wild stallions galloping across the prairie.

"You are E. Love, aren't you? Does it stand for Evangeline or Emily? It doesn't rightly matter, so long as you'll be my wife." He grabbed her hand in his sweaty palm.

She swallowed past a lump in her throat. "I think there's been some sort of misunderstanding."

His busy eyebrows drew together. "Aren't you in need of a husband? It says so right here." He tugged a newspaper clipping from his pocket.

Essie glanced toward the back room, where her sisters were hopefully not overhearing her conversation with the stranger. "Yes, but I've changed my mind." Surely, she could have *some* say in who she married. This man certainly didn't fit into the picture she had in mind.

The husband she'd envisioned would be tall, dark-haired, with a twinkle in his eyes every time he smiled at her. A hardworking man—not afraid to get his hands in the dirt, but gentle with a wife and children. That's the kind of fellow she desired to spend her life with, but she found herself needing a fill-in husband who could provide for the financial needs of Essie and her sisters. Not that she had a lick of desire to be bound to any man. If Pa hadn't left them in such a bind...

The man cleared his throat and frowned at her. "If you didn't want a mate, then why did you advertise for one?"

She shrugged and opened the door, cold air swirling into the room. "I'm sorry to have inconvenienced you."

He sputtered and jammed a derby hat on, grumbling under his breath as he left.

She refrained from slamming the door behind him. Instead, Essie turned and rested her back against it for a moment, trying to calm the erratic pulsing of her heart.

Kitty poked her head out of Pa's room and studied her. "Who was that?" She edged closer.

"Nobody of consequence." Essie squeezed Kitty's shoulder as she moved past her. "Does Teddy need anything?"

"What? Oh, yes, she sent me out to get a pan of cool water to bathe his face and bring down the fever." Kitty motioned toward the pump.

"Why don't you let me take care of that, and you can start breakfast? You always were the best cook of all of us." Essie prayed her sister would be easily distracted, like normal, and not ask anything further about the unexpected visitor Essie had shooed away.

"Thank you, Es, you're the best." Kitty gave her a quick hug before reaching for her coat. "I'll go see if the chickens laid anything yet."

Essie breathed easier once her sister closed the door behind her.

She poured water from the pitcher into the basin and threw a small cloth into it as well.

Teddy wouldn't be as easy to fool.

Her hands trembled as she stepped into Pa's room.

"There you are. If you can take over here, I best see to the animals." Teddy shoved away from the side of the bed and shifted past her.

Whew. She certainly hadn't thought it would be *that* easy. *Thank You, Lord.* She set the basin on the nightstand beside the bed and wrung out the cloth, placing it on the man's feverish forehead. As she positioned it, she shifted his unruly blonde waves out of the way. Her fingers lingered for a second over the coarseness of the textured locks. She startled when a rumble sounded from his throat.

"How long are you planning on playing with my hair, Angel?"

Jud's fuzzy thoughts couldn't recall whether the one stroking his hair was the angel or the evil one. Or had it all been a dream? This one didn't have her ringlets down her back anymore, but had her hair pulled tight into a bun at the nape of her neck. If she was the beauty, he'd witnessed the night before, he'd much rather see her with her hair free around her slim waist, flowing and soft looking.

"You're awake." She adjusted the cloth. "How are you feeling?"

If you reward me with a smile, I'll be the happiest man around. He shifted on the bed and bit back a moan. "Fair."

"How did you get shot?" Her blue eyes felt as if they pierced straight through him.

He pinched his lips tight. Why'd she have to go and ruin things by starting their conversation like that?

She stood with hands thrust on her hips. "Not wanting to talk about it, huh? I don't know who you are, mister, but you better not bring any trouble to my sisters and me. You hear?"

Sisters. So, it hadn't been a dream. They were the ones who had taken care of him. He couldn't resist lifting the blanket and peeking beneath it. He gasped. *A dress?* Where were his pants?

His gaze lifted, and color flooded across the woman's cheeks. Did he have any dignity left?

"We figured you'd be more comfortable in Pa's nightshirt." Her voice faltered, and her gaze dipped. If they weren't talking about this particular topic, he'd laugh at her nervousness. He couldn't recall the last time he had had a woman interested in him. His leg wound must have addled his brain as well. Jud shook his head.

He glanced around the small room. She'd mentioned a pa. Where was he, and why hadn't the man taken care of him instead? Jud shivered. "It's cold in here."

She flew out of the room but soon returned with a fancy quilt covered in flowers. It smelled like them, too. When she tucked it around his frame, he realized it smelled like *her*. Had she taken it from her own bed? His cheeks flamed at the thought. He needed to get better and away from this house full of women. They threw him off kilter. Give him the open range, Buster beneath him, and... His pulse stalled. "Buster? What happened to him?"

"Who? We found only you last night." She flipped over the cloth on his forehead, and it sent a chill down his spine.

"My horse."

"I'm sure Teddy will find him if he hasn't wandered off by now." She tucked the blanket under his chin as if he were a child. It kind of felt good. Something he could take a liking to. Was this what it would feel like to have a wife fussing over him?

He shivered and hunkered lower under the covers. Best to keep his mind on the topic at hand. "Buster wouldn't wander off."

"Kitty," the beauty hollered. "Run out and see if Teddy found the man's horse."

A door thudded moments later.

"You never told me your name." Her gaze met his.

"Neither did you."

Her cheeks blossomed again. He kind of liked it.

"It's Essie, I mean Esther. My sisters are Kit and

Theodora."

Who named their daughters with male names? Well, at least close to one's fellas usually had. "Angel, do you think you could take the rag off my head? It's making me colder." He couldn't stop the shivers from convulsing his body.

"My name isn't Angel. I told you. I'm Essie."

"Sure, Angel, whatever you say."

She glowered at him, and he couldn't stop the chuckle that burst forth. Angel looked even prettier when she was riled. He'd have to see what else he could do to make her irritated when he felt up to it. "Where's your pa?"

Her hand faltered for a split second before she steadied it. "He's no longer with us."

He held her gaze for a moment. If he weren't so cold, he'd reach for her hand. He shook the notion aside. "I'm sorry. Losing family members is never easy." He should know. Other than his foolish cousin, he had no other relatives living.

"Both he and Ma are gone. I'm the one who has to make sure my sisters are taken care of now." She bit her lip as if she'd said more than she'd wanted to.

He yawned. "Keep that evil sister of yours away from me, and we'll be good. If you don't mind, Angel, I think I could use a little shuteye. Wake me for the next watch so I can keep track of the doggies. We don't want any cattle rustlers coming in and stealing them."

Her jaw dropped before she sputtered like spilled coffee dancing on a hot cookstove top. It was the finest thing he'd ever seen. He couldn't stop a smile from breaking free.

CHAPTER FOUR

D aylight pierced through Jud's closed eyelids like knives stabbing his skin. He squinted against the streams of sunshine and dragged a shaky hand across his jaw. His fingers traced the bottom portion of his face covered in hair. Since when had he grown a beard? He'd always prided himself on being clean-shaven each morning, even on cattle drives.

Once his eyes adjusted to the brightness of the room, his arms trembled like a newborn calf as he hiked his body higher in the bed. Where was he, and why was he in bed in the middle of the day?

Whispered voices outside the room drew his attention.

"What are we going to do if he dies?" A gentle voice sounded somewhat familiar. Was there concern in it? He didn't know a single soul who'd care what happened to him. She must be talking about someone else.

"We don't even know his name." Another woman's voice joined the first. This one was a little deeper. "I can't believe you told him your name, but didn't find out who he is."

His forehead wrinkled.

"Don't be hard on her, Teddy." A lilting tone came from a different lady.

How had he wound up in a household of at least three females? Heaven help him if there were even more. He shook his head. Why couldn't he remember what had happened? Had they drugged him? No medicine bottles stood on the nightstand beside the bed, but one of them could have hidden it somewhere.

"You need to get some sleep today, Essie. You've been near his bedside for weeks."

Weeks? They were talking about him. It explained the beard. He couldn't remember how he'd gotten here. Wherever *here* was. Snatches of that evening filtered back. The cold and snowy night. The memory of the ripping pain through his body from a gunshot wound. He'd tried to find help before rolling down a briar-covered embankment.

Shoes scraped across the wooden floorboards, pulling him back to the present. Three female heads poked through the doorway. Each with the same broad forehead and brilliant blue eyes. They had to be sisters. Two were brown-haired and the other towhead. The one dressed like a fella and the blonde stumbled over each other as they entered the room. The third lingered in the doorway. Dark shadows smudged the skin beneath her eyes. Could she be Essie? Was that the name of his angel?

The rough one stepped closer to the bed and ran a hand across his forehead. Thick calluses caught in his hair.

"Is he still feverish, Teddy?" Worry lined the angel's face.

The woman beside him shook her head. "Nope. We need to change the dressin' again though."

The blonde blanched. "Maybe I should see about some broth if he feels up to it."

"Make sure it's a clear one, Kitty. His belly won't be able to stomach any proper food after goin' without solids for nearly three weeks."

The squeamish one vacated the room like a rabbit being chased by a hound dog. He hoped she'd return with something to eat.

His stomach growled as if to prove its hollowness. He tried to lick his dry lips.

The angel seemed to sense his predicament. She stepped into the room, snagged a pitcher and poured water into a glass before she made her way to the bed.

A beverage had never looked so refreshing.

Her gaze met his for a second before she brought the glass to his lips.

He drank thirstily, but only for a few seconds before she pulled it away. A droplet spilled from his mouth. He tried to swipe it with his hand, but his body refused to cooperate. His angel's feather-light finger wiped his lip, branding it with her touch. He swallowed as prickles ran the length of his arms, stirring something in him he'd never experienced before.

She wouldn't meet his gaze, but the one called Teddy hadn't stopped scrutinizing him since his angel had touched his mouth.

"You don't want to put too much in your stomach until we see how you do." Angel's words were a welcome break from her sister's staring contest.

He bit back a chuckle. Didn't Angel know a fella could go a few days without a meal and then eat a juicy steak without his belly complaining?

Pink tinged the tips of her ears. "We've been worried about you. You've been out of your mind for weeks with a high fever and an infection."

What had he said? How much did they know about him and his past? They hadn't kicked him out, so maybe that was a good sign.

Teddy stepped closer to the bed and folded her arms across her chest. She pinned him with a glare. "Who are you, mister, and how did you find yourself with a bullet in your leg?"

Essie leaned forward, awaiting the man's response. He'd said many things when he'd tossed and turned while his body fought off the infection, but never his name.

A low rumble came from his throat. "Name's Judah."

A Bible name. It suited him, although she couldn't picture a cowboy having such a fine one. As much as he'd talked about cattle, rustlers, and riding the range, his chosen profession had been obvious—probably a drifter who went from ranch to ranch looking for work. Unstable. Not the kind of man she needed. Never mind that she'd been unable to keep him from her thoughts as she'd cared for him night and day.

Teddy had kept busy tending to the needs of the farm while Kitty maintained their home and provided the meals. Between bouts of nursing Judah, Essie had worked on an idea for a new book, but the hero kept turning into a villain. She sighed and hid her ink-stained hands, not needing the constant reminder of how she'd failed her sisters. Only five weeks remained before they'd lose all they held dear—unless God somehow intervened.

"Were you plannin' on sharin' how you got shot?" Teddy hovered over the bed like a vulture ready to pounce on its prey. "For all we know, we could be harborin' a fugitive."

Something flickered across Judah's face, but he remained tight-lipped. His eyes fluttered closed, and his body slumped. Essie wondered if he faked being asleep.

Teddy snorted and turned on her heel. "See what you can get out of him when he wakes. I'd best go take care of the critters. Looks like another storm'll be blowin' through later tonight. I need to tie a rope from the house to the barn in case the snow piles up again. Call if you need me." She jammed Pa's old hat on her head. "Don't forget to change that dressin'. You might want to take care of it while he's sleepin'."

Essie nodded and then turned to study Judah. Not a single muscle flickered in his long frame. She crossed the room, lifted the small crate of supplies, and set it on the dresser. Then she uncorked the bottle of alcohol and dabbed it on the new bandages Kitty had cut earlier.

Swallowing, she flipped back the covers and took a deep breath. It had been hard enough to take care of Judah's needs while he lay in a fevered state, but now that he was in his right mind again, she had a difficult time bringing herself to the task at hand. Her fingers shook as she unwound the strips around his leg. Finally, the packing gave way. She peered at the area. Everything appeared to be healing nicely. At least the pus had finally gone away.

Essie dropped the old bandages in a bucket and pressed the alcohol-soaked cloth against his now cool skin. A sharp intake of breath caused her to stop her ministrations.

His eyes flickered beneath his eyelids, but they didn't open. She released a small breath when he didn't stir again and finished the task at hand. Easing the blanket back in place, she tugged it over his chest, her hand lingering there for a second longer than necessary. Did his cheeks look flushed again? She couldn't tell for sure.

Essie's emotions warred within her. Taking care of Judah had stirred unwanted feelings and thoughts. The last time her heart had fluttered, it'd been when her ex-fiancé had kissed her. But Timothy Miller's chaste kiss when he'd proposed to her, followed by his betrayal when he'd called off their engagement, was in the past. As soon as he'd learned the financial state she was in, he'd spouted that he had no interest in being saddled with three women. So much for true love conquering obstacles. Hogwash!

How could she ever write love stories for women when she knew the truth? Men were unpredictable and contemptible. She wouldn't allow herself to be hornswoggled by another—not if she could help it. She'd be in charge of her destiny and future. Marriage would only be for convenience's sake and for saving the farm. Nothing else.

CHAPTER FIVE

J ud lay as still as possible. Not a single muscle twitched, except when his angel had placed something cold that bit like a hornet's sting on his upper thigh. He didn't dare open his eyes, or she'd start questioning him about how he got the wound in the first place, and he had no intention of sharing that. The sooner he got better, the sooner he could be on his way. Far away, where he couldn't bring harm to them, where the scent of flowers and the touch of a beautiful woman didn't stir his senses.

He prayed she hadn't seen the sudden flush in his cheeks. If anything, she'd think he had a fever again. Hopefully, she'd leave the room soon so he could work on exercising his limbs and getting strong once more. He felt as weak as a newborn colt standing for the first time, and he hadn't even stood yet. Maybe after a few moments of shut-eye he'd feel more like himself.

When he opened his eyes again sometime later, shadows stretched across the room, making it difficult to see. The scent of stewed chicken set his mouth watering. A voice cleared, and he heard the strike of a match before a light flared.

His angel yawned and dropped the globe into place on the kerosene lamp. "Looks like we both got some rest." A smile tugged at her full lips. "If you're feeling up to it, I'm sure Kitty has that broth ready by now. If you're interested."

He nodded, not trusting his voice. Seeming to read his thoughts, she slid one arm under his head and brought a glass to his lips with the other. This time she let him drink his fill. His stomach gurgled with the fresh addition to it.

"Good, you two are awake." The blonde entered the room with a steaming bowl. "I thought I heard you talking." She set the bowl on the nightstand. "Are you feeling any better, Judah?"

"I will once I get some food in me." His voice was husky from lack of use.

Her face softened. "I can read you one of Essie's stories while she feeds you."

He opened his mouth to say that he could feed himself, but the beauty who'd been caring for him interrupted.

"I'm sure he doesn't want to hear my drivel, Kitty." Angel fiddled with her hands for a second before rearranging items on the dresser.

He narrowed his gaze. What kind of work did she do to cause the black stains on them?

"Nonsense. What man doesn't love hearing about a romance?" Kitty tucked a blonde lock behind her ear. "I have one of your stories here, Essie." She whipped out some sort of magazine.

A man and woman stood on the front cover holding hands. *Belles & Beaux*. It was the only thing he saw before Angel ripped the publication from her sister's grasp.

Kitty's lip protruded, and he bit back a laugh at the woman's fake pout. She yanked the journal back. "You feed him, and I'll read."

"Kit." Angel's voice rose a notch.

"What?" The blonde turned innocent eyes toward her sister before she shifted her gaze to him. "Wouldn't you like to hear what my sister wrote?"

His curiosity piqued, he nodded, finding himself very interested in learning how his angel thought. Her being his sole caretaker for the past few weeks had him wondering what kind of woman she was. Maybe hearing something she wrote would give him a better idea of what thoughts ran through her head.

He didn't take time to ponder why it mattered to him.

Angel shifted her seat closer, picked up the bowl and spoon, and sat down with a *humph*. Dark eyelashes fluttered against her pale skin.

Kitty cleared her throat and sat at the foot of his bed. *"Evangeline Richard's heart pattered like a drum, vibrating with each step that Leroy King took closer to her. Could he hear it? Would he ever think of her as more than the girl he climbed trees with when they were mere youths?"*

Jud slurped another spoonful of broth from his angel, his brow puckering as Kitty sighed, clasping the magazine against her chest for a second. Did women really think like that? He glanced back at Angel, but she wouldn't meet his eyes. Did *she* think that way? She must have, since she wrote it.

The warmth of the broth surged through his body. He hadn't been so well taken care of since he'd been a boy. Ma had died shortly before his tenth birthday and Pa soon afterward. Not wanting to stay with his rowdy cousin's family, Jud had lit out on his own, looking for a job on any ranch that would take him. Pa had taught him how to handle horses, and he'd gotten his first job doing that. A local ranch owner had two horses that had taken sick, and Jud had known how to care for them.

His wandering reflections caused him to miss part of the story Kitty was reading, but Angel's eyes didn't miss a thing. Something flickered across her face. He hoped she wouldn't assume he'd lost interest. A sigh slipped past her lips as she shoveled another spoonful of broth between his.

"I think he's heard enough, Kitty. If you fix me a plate, I'll be out in a few minutes."

Kitty stopped mid-sentence. "I can read more to you while Essie eats." A grin spread across her face as she winked at him. "I'll be back."

"Not with that story." His angel ground the words out. What had caused such bitterness in her life? He bet her sister would share the tale if he sweet-talked her.

Essie shoved the food back and forth across her plate. Why did Kitty have to remind her of that terrible story? She'd written it when Timothy had first taken notice of her. What a besotted fool she'd been.

She stabbed a bite of chicken and jammed it into her mouth. The tines of the fork scraped against the inside of her cheek. She pushed the plate back, crossed to the window, and stared out. Snow had already coated the ground. Essie shivered as the wind whistled around the chimney. So much for slipping to town to see if any letters had come for her in care of the newspaper office. Even if the storm raged tomorrow, she'd have to find a way to get there. Her heart pinched tighter with each passing day.

With Judah being so sick, she hadn't been able to get away from the house without her sisters demanding an explanation. Since the cowboy had taken a turn for the better, perhaps she could come up with the excuse of needing to go outdoors to stretch her legs. It wouldn't work for her to trek into town at night because the office would have closed already, but come the next morning she'd make her way there.

She had to sell a story soon too. Going back to the table, she dropped into her seat and shifted a piece of paper closer, along with her pen and inkwell. The scritch of the pen against the paper made her feel like she was being productive, but lately her pages were filled with smudges from where she crossed out words, or else they lay in a crumpled mess at her feet. She *had* to come up with an idea that would make a good story. She prayed it would happen soon, before it was too late.

Teddy opened the door, and a blast of frigid air and snowflakes flew into the room. She stamped the snow from her boots and brushed ice from her hat. "Brr. We're in for a bad one. I could barely see to get back from the barn. With the wind pickin' up, it'll be driftin' somethin' fierce by mornin'." She shrugged out of her coat and hung it on a hook near the door, then blew on her hands. "I think this is the first I've seen you out of Pa's room. I'm guessin' the stranger is doin' better?"

Essie yawned and shifted the pages aside. "I fed him a bowl of broth. He drank the whole thing."

"Looks like he ate more than you did." Teddy's brows hiked. "You feelin' peaked?"

"I'm fine. There's no need to worry about me." Essie brushed a piece of lint from the sleeve of her blue dress.

Teddy didn't answer, but Essie could feel her sister's gaze drilling into her.

"Somethin' on your mind?" Teddy moved closer, and Essie jumped up to fix a plate of food for her youngest sister.

"Why would there be?" She lifted the lid off the warm pot. The scent of herbs and chicken wafted up, causing her stomach to growl.

"Caught another fella sniffin' 'round the barn."

The metal fork she'd used to pierce a piece of chicken clattered to the floor. She bent to retrieve it. "Oh?"

Teddy shifted a step closer to her. "Yes. He isn't the first one either."

"H-how many?" She hated the way her voice trembled. Surely her sister would notice. "What have they been looking for?" She glanced down at her shoes. Teddy's were right against hers. She swallowed and finally glanced up to meet her sister's narrowed eyes.

"Five. And they've all been lookin' for you."

That many? Would they come back again, or had Teddy scared them off?

"What's goin' on, Essie? I think it's time you let me in on what's been houndin' you."

CHAPTER SIX

J ud moved a checker across the board. Angel nibbled on her lip as she contemplated her next move. He almost lifted his hand to halt her chawing, but stopped himself before she noticed. Her tongue snaked out as she licked her lips. He forced himself to look away. Each time he witnessed her nervous action, it stirred something in his gut. Something he didn't want to examine and discover what it was.

After a bit of convincing, the sisters had finally allowed him to be up and sitting in a chair. He felt weaker than a newborn bird, but he wouldn't let them know that. Jud shifted his position.

"Are you uncomfortable?" Angel's eyes darkened as she studied his face. "Perhaps we should get you back to bed."

He waved away her concerns. "I'm fine. Are you going to make a move, or what?"

She studied him for a moment before she glanced back at the board and shifted a piece.

"Who's winning?" Kitty glanced up from the checkerboard she shared with Teddy.

Jud lifted a shoulder. "Nobody yet. How about you two?"

Teddy grinned at him. "That would be me. Kitty's never had a head for strategy."

He couldn't help chuckling.

Kitty tipped her head to the side and surveyed him for a minute. He held himself still. "I think you are a fine man, Judah."

Fire filled his cheeks, and when he caught sight of Angel, roses filled hers as well. His heart thudded in his ears. Why was Angel bothered by what her sister had said? Was it possible Angel had an interest in him?

Silence stretched.

"Er, thank you, Kitty." Jud ducked his head and moved a round disk without really looking at the board.

Angel jumped several of his pieces and removed them.

His gaze settled on the window. Outside, the wind and snow blew against the glass pane. He didn't miss being outside in this kind of weather. In fact, he could get used to the life of a farmer. Maybe even... He shook the notion aside.

"You *are* feeling poorly." Angel stood. "We need to get you back to bed."

"Stop your hoverin', Essie. You're worse than a mother hen watchin' over her chicks." Teddy shoved a piece of popcorn in her mouth and chewed. "It does a man good to be up and about. Besides, his body won't ever strengthen if he stays in bed." She waggled her eyebrows at him.

"Yes, but..." Angel's hand dropped to his shoulder before

she snatched it away like she'd been burned. Flames blazed up her neck and splashed across her face.

He reached up and snagged her hand. "I'm fine, Angel. Really. Sit down so we can finish our game."

She stared at their clasped hands.

Kitty giggled.

Angel's eyes flew open, and she tugged her hand away. She bustled over to the table and scooped some popcorn into a bowl.

Teddy watched Jud's every movement. Was this what it felt like to be part of a family? Had he missed out on all this? What would his life have been like if his parents had lived and he'd had additional siblings? He wouldn't be in this situation. That was for sure. But he couldn't help but thank the Good Lord that He'd brought him to Angel's door. Jud couldn't stop a grin from spreading.

Teddy's gaze narrowed. "Wha'cha thinkin' about, cowboy?"

"Family. You're blessed to have each other." Sudden moisture clogged his throat.

Something softened on Teddy's face as she inspected him. "Maybe you aren't so bad after all."

His heart swelled.

Essie listened to the exchange between Judah and Teddy. Teddy typically guarded herself against opening up to folks. That she'd just given her approval of Judah surprised

Essie. She didn't know what to do with the information.

She set the bowl of popcorn next to Judah and settled across from him. Obviously, his thoughts hadn't been on the game. She could beat him in two more moves. Would it offend his male ego if she won? Why did she care how he felt?

The quicker this snow stopped and she could make it into town, the better off she'd be. Hopefully, some letters awaited her, and she could think about something else other than the man she'd been tending to.

She supposed it was natural that they would start having inklings of feelings for each other. But their attachment likely stemmed from her care for him these past weeks. Hadn't she read somewhere about patients falling for the nurses who assisted in their healing? She soon would be a distant memory for him, and she could get on with the business of saving her family. So why did the notion leave her feeling empty inside?

CHAPTER SEVEN

E ssie shivered against the cold seeping into her bones. Diamonds sparkled in the sun, shining on the waist-high snowdrifts. She trudged one weary step after another, plodding slow progress to town. So much for making it there and back home again before her sisters awakened. She should've left them a note.

The conversation with Teddy from a week ago played through her mind. Her sister had been suspicious when she'd told her about advertising for a husband. Essie hadn't mentioned why she needed one, and Teddy hadn't asked. She'd let the matter drop, probably too exhausted from having worked in the barn.

On Pa's deathbed, he'd tasked Essie with keeping watch over her sisters and making sure she cared for them. There was no way she'd let Pa down. It was her responsibility as the oldest to provide for them.

Essie rubbed the tight muscles in her neck. She needed a husband who could cover her debt to the bank and soon.

At least until she sold a story. If only a new idea would take shape in her mind.

She blew out a breath, the puff of mist breaking the serene scene. It had snowed every day over the past week, making it impossible for her to get to town sooner. They'd played games every night. After the initial match with Judah, she made sure they hadn't been paired together again.

Rubbing her hands together and blowing on her knit mittens, she sighed with relief when the newspaper office finally came into view.

The owner withdrew a key from his pocket and shoved the door open. "Hello there, Essie. I didn't expect anyone to be moving about on this chilly morning. I got a pile of letters for you." He chuckled, his brown eyes sparkling. "Looks like you'll have your pick of the litter."

She followed him into his shop. The scent of paper and ink filled her nostrils, and she breathed it in deeply. She'd never grow tired of the smell. "I'll take a copy of this week's paper too."

Mr. Brown trudged to the big wooden counter and reached across to the cubbyholes, withdrawing a stack of letters. "Here you go." He plopped them down and turned to get a newspaper from the bundle on the floor beside the printing press. "Anything else?"

Essie shook her head and handed him a coin. "Thank you."

"You be careful on your way home. There's talk all over the territory about a wanted man. Have heard little about it, but I aim to learn more. You'll see a picture of him in the paper you've got there. Name's Steele."

A shiver scurried up Essie's spine. She swallowed. Judah had never shared his last name or how he had received his gunshot wound. Were they harboring a criminal?

She tucked the letters and newspaper into her satchel. "Thank you. Good day."

Her curiosity piqued, she forced herself to wait until she was far beyond the town limits before she peeked at the newspaper. There, splayed across the front page, was the story of a J. Steele, wanted for a stagecoach robbery, bank theft, and murder. Her blood ran cold at the last word, and she nearly dropped the periodical. The sketch beside the article didn't give a clear picture of what the man looked like. She squinted. It kind of resembled Judah, but she couldn't tell for sure. His face had been so bruised when he first arrived, and a beard had since covered half of it.

Dear Lord, keep us safe. A verse she'd read from the Gospel of Luke played through her mind.

'But love ye your enemies, and do good, and lend, hoping for nothing again; and your reward shall be great, and ye shall be the children of the Highest: for he is kind unto the unthankful and to the evil.'

Is that what You're asking of us, Lord? To be kind to Judah? But what happens if he turns out to be a reprobate? Will we be guilty too because of our association with him?

She mulled it over the entire way home and still hadn't reached an answer when the door to the house flew open.

"Where have you been? Your sisters have been worried sick." Judah swayed on his feet and then slumped into a snowdrift.

Jud woke to a gaggle of women clucking and hovering like a hen atop her brood of chicks. He shivered. Something wet soaked through his pant leg.

"What were you thinkin'?" Teddy grumbled under her breath. If she were a fella, she likely would've punched him, as angry as she looked. "Probably busted open your wound."

"We need to get him out of the snow." Kitty pushed closer, wringing her hands.

Angel arrived breathless, shoving her way past her sisters. "What kind of fool are you?"

A grin broke across his face. "Apparently not as big a one as you are for walking to town in this weather."

Her face pinched.

Oops. Too late, he realized womenfolk might not take teasing as well as a cowpoke could.

"You sure about that, Steele?"

His mouth went dry. Where had she heard *that* name? It couldn't be a coincidence. Maybe she only called him that to see if he'd fall into her trap.

He braced himself. Not if he could help it.

He schooled his features or at least hoped he had. "I don't know what you're talking about, Angel. Told you my name's Judah."

Her lips puckered together as if she'd sucked on a lemon.

"I don't know what's goin' on between you two, but we need to get this fool back to bed before he undoes all your care over the past month." Teddy flung Jud's arm around her neck. "Essie, get on his other side to help him up, and Kitty hang onto the back of his shirt so he don't go pitchin' forward and take us all with him."

A sheen of sweat soaked his body by the time they got him sprawled across the bed again.

Teddy scowled at the blood soaking through his britches.

He held up a hand. "I can take care of it myself this time." It might not happen until the next day, but they didn't need to know that. Every ounce of his energy had been spent pulling on a pair of pants earlier and hobbling the short distance between his room and outside. The first time he'd walked unassisted.

The girls were right. It had been a fool's errand, but when Angel hadn't shown up with his breakfast and he'd heard her sisters' low voices of concern coming from their bedroom, he hadn't been able to hold back any longer. Not that he'd have had the strength to make it any further than the barn, let alone trying to saddle his horse, but he'd been ready to try.

"You'll do no such thing." Angel's arms folded over her chest. "You two, shoo. I'll take care of him."

Teddy eye-balled her sister. "Once you do that, we need to talk. Like Judah said, he isn't the only one not usin' sense today."

Angel's gaze dropped, and she fumbled with some sort of bag. She hung it on the bedpost. "I'll wash my hands and be right back."

Something important had to be in the bag to make her walk all the way to town and back in these conditions. As soon as they all left the room, he ripped the satchel from its spot and opened it. Out dropped a stack of letters and a newspaper. The paper fell open, and his face—or rather his cousin's—stared back at him. *She knew*. Or at least, she'd put some pieces together, even if they weren't exactly accurate.

His hand caught on one of the envelopes. A man's handwriting. Why would a fella be writing to his angel? He couldn't resist peeking at them. Each missive held a different male's script, and all addressed to E. Love. It had to be her. Interesting last name. She'd never shared it before.

Why would so many men be corresponding with her? A boulder settled in his gut. Surely, she didn't need a husband or anything like that. Why should he care if she hitched herself to a fella? It wasn't like he could plant roots down here. If he ever did though, he'd consider a woman like her—beauty and feistiness all wrapped together into a nice package.

Jud blew out a breath and shoved everything inside the bag. He'd just sat back against the headboard after removing his pants and smoothing the ridiculous nightshirt in place when Angel came through the door with a basin of steaming water. He prayed she wouldn't notice his throbbing heart or guess what he'd been up to in her absence.

She set the basin down. Her fingers shook as she wrung out a cloth.

Jud shifted the sheet so only his seeping wound was exposed, sucking air in through his teeth when she dabbed the area. What else had she placed on the rag?

"You'll live, so long as you don't do something stupid

like that again." She was none too gentle with cleaning the wound and re-wrapping it. "What were you thinking, walking outside in this kind of weather?"

"Exactly. What were *you* thinking, walking to town when the snowdrifts were waist deep?" He breathed easier once she'd covered his leg back with the blanket.

She scowled at him.

"Did you have mail you had to get?" He realized too late he should've kept his mouth shut.

Her eyes narrowed, and she glanced at her satchel near the foot of the bed.

"Did you have something you wanted to share with me?" Angel paused. "Like your last name?"

CHAPTER EIGHT

E ssie tried to outstare Judah, but failed. A persistent knocking at the door interrupted her silent battle with the insufferable man. She huffed, leaving the room as the noise continued. Her sisters were nowhere to be seen as she entered the kitchen and swung the door open.

A tall, dark-haired man stood, his hat at a jaunty angle and a broad smile splitting his chiseled face. He bowed, reached for her hand, and brought her fingers to his lips.

Her heart fluttered at his chivalrous act.

"Might you be E. Love?"

"Yes, I'm Esther. Won't you please come in?" She opened the door wider.

"I'm pleased to meet you, Miss Love. My name is Benjamin Wilcox. I sent you a couple of letters but hadn't received a response." A smile tugged at his cheek muscles again. "I hope you don't find my showing up on your doorstep presumptuous. The mail can be so unreliable, I thought I'd best come introduce myself in case my correspondence hadn't arrived."

"We've had an awful week of snowstorms, and I only got to town this morning to pick up my mail." Essie motioned him toward a chair at the table. "I haven't had the chance to read any of it yet. Please have a seat while I warm the pot of coffee. You must be cold after coming all this way. Where did you say you're from?"

"I don't think he mentioned it yet, Angel." Judah's eyes twinkled as he joined Mr. Wilcox at the table. "Name's Judah. Like in the Bible."

The caller nodded, and the men shook hands.

She wanted to punch Judah. Why couldn't he stay in Pa's room?

Mr. Wilcox's gaze traveled back and forth between Essie and Judah, his forehead puckering. "Is this your brother?"

"Absolutely not!" She jammed her hands onto her hips.

Judah grinned. "Nope. I'm here visiting my *good* friends." When she came close to him, he looped an arm around her waist.

Essie resisted the urge to stomp on his foot. "Shouldn't you lie down and rest?"

"Nope. Figured I won't build up my strength staying abed most of the day."

The stranger gave her a confused look. "I can see I've come at a bad time."

"Nonsense. I'm glad you're here." She set a cup of coffee in front of him. "I have cream and sugar if you'd like."

He shook his head. "No need. I take it black."

"You know the way I like it." Judah winked and patted her hand. "I think you forgot a cup for me though, Angel."

Essie snatched her hand away and rose to fetch a cup for him. Maybe he'd leave her alone with Mr. Wilcox once Judah had drunk his coffee.

She plunked the mug in front of him, splashing the dark brown liquid onto his hand. Essie cringed. As upset as she was with Judah, she'd not intended to harm him.

The man didn't even wince.

Essie huffed and perched on a chair, arranging the folds of her skirt, which were still damp from her trek to town. She shivered. "Why don't you tell me about yourself, Mr. Wilcox?"

Judah stood and limped toward the peg where her shawl hung, grabbed it, and slowly made his way across the kitchen before he draped it around her shoulders. His fingers lingered at her neck longer than necessary, and the warmth from his hand remained long after he'd settled back in his chair.

Mr. Wilcox frowned as he blew across his coffee. He took a sip. "Please call me Benjamin." His lips twitched. "Especially since I hope our lives will be joined in marriage soon." He took another slurp of his hot drink. "I'm a banker in the Dallas area—"

"Did you say banker?" Her whole body stiffened, and she felt the color drain from her face.

The stranger nodded, not noticing her disquiet, and plodded on. "Things are booming there, since we have two train routes now. I can more than adequately provide for a wife."

Leave Kansas? She'd placed the advertisement for someone willing to help her save the farmstead. *Would he consider settling here?* "I suppose the type of work you have at the bank is something you could do wherever you lived."

Benjamin rubbed his chin. "Possibly, but I've no desire to leave Texas. Doesn't the Good Book say a wife is to follow her husband?"

"In the book of Genesis, it says for a *man* to leave his parents and cleave to his wife." Judah pinned the banker with a stare.

Essie's cheeks flamed.

Judah tilted his wooden chair back on two legs. "Maybe you're thinking of the story of Ruth when she said she'd go wherever her mother-in-law Naomi went. She said, 'for whither thou goest, I will go; and where thou lodgest, I will lodge: thy people shall be my people, and thy God my God.' Then again, perhaps you haven't read that story in the Bible."

Essie shot a glance at Jud. The cowboy definitely knew his Scriptures.

Benjamin's face flushed. "I'm afraid my schedule doesn't always allow time for Bible reading."

What did that mean? Her advertisement specifically mentioned desiring a man of faith. "There must be many churches in Dallas."

He nodded. "You'll have your choice."

Essie nibbled on the dry skin on her lip. Judah's presence made it impossible to ask some questions she needed to know the answer to. Why couldn't he take a hint and go away? She tried darting a silent message his way.

Jud bit back a grin. Angel clearly wanted him to leave her alone with the scoundrel, but something didn't ring true with the banker, and he aimed to find out what it was.

Her face had said a lot when the visitor mentioned his profession. For some reason, she had an aversion to it. Maybe he could dig deeper and find more things she'd dislike about the stranger. "Have you been in Dallas long?"

Benjamin's eyes narrowed. "A few years. What line of work are you in?" The man met his gaze. "You strike me as a cowboy or drifter. Definitely *not* what Miss Love is interested in."

That sounded like a challenge.

Angel's cheeks turned rosy. The way Jud liked them. If he did anything before he left, he'd make sure she and her sisters were provided for. It was the least he could do after the many kindnesses they'd shown him.

Benjamin shifted his attention back to Angel. "Your notice in the paper said you preferred a marriage of convenience by April fourteenth. That's an entire month away, my dear. I'd hoped we'd wed immediately, so we could travel back to Texas as man and wife. I have only a few days before I must be back."

Angel sputtered, and her eyes darted a look at Jud again before resting on Benjamin. "I would need to learn more about you, and I had planned to stay here with my two sisters."

"Sisters? You never mentioned sisters. Why can't they stay

here without you?" The banker surveyed the small room.

Angel licked her lips and ran her fingernail along a crack in the wooden table. "They can't."

Jud considered Angel's response, studying her expression. There was more to her tale. Did she not share it with the stranger because Jud was present, or did something else deter her? Something to do with her distaste of bankers? He'd not rest until he found out.

CHAPTER NINE

G ood riddance. Jud had thought the banker would never leave. Sitting in the straight-backed chair for hours, listening to the man ramble on and on about himself, had Jud's body aching something fierce. He longed for the comfort of the bed, but he had a small window of time to get answers before Angel's sisters returned from wherever they'd gone.

Angel dropped her hand from the latch. When she turned back toward him, Jud couldn't identify the emotion in her expression. "You aren't considering his proposition, are you?"

She cleared her throat but didn't answer him right away. "Not that it's your concern, but I wanted to stay here, with Kitty and Teddy."

"Why can't you? You don't need a man to live here. You three seem to do fine on your own." Maybe he could convince her to give up the idea of marriage altogether. Well, at least to that scoundrel.

She shook her head. "You don't understand."

"Then tell me, so I do."

Her fingers wound around the tassels on her shawl. "I can't."

"Something's been troubling you, Angel. You might as well spill it, since you haven't confided in Teddy or Kitty."

Her gaze darted toward his, color seeping from her cheeks. "How do you know that?"

"Because you wouldn't have sent for a man if you could have solved the problem without others coming to your aid. As protective as your sisters are, they would've helped you come up with a plan to face whatever the obstacle is." He stood and limped toward her.

"You really should get back in bed." She wouldn't meet his eyes.

"I will. After you tell me what's going on."

"Why?" She crossed her arms. "You haven't told me anything about you, and it's been over a month since I found you."

"I promise I will, but first let's solve your problem."

Emotions warred on her face. "You'll tell me what's going on and who you really are?"

Jud heaved a sigh. If she'd talk to him, it'd be worth it. He nodded.

She nibbled her cracked lips.

He placed his finger on them to halt her movements. They trembled beneath his touch.

Her eyes widened.

It took every ounce of determination not to find out what they tasted like. Something he'd been thinking about all week. Instead, he clasped her hand and pulled her toward a chair. He made sure he settled a good five feet away from her so he wouldn't be tempted to touch her again.

Angel sat for several minutes, not saying a word. "The bank's going to foreclose on our home unless I come up with a hundred dollars to pay off the mortgage."

He whistled. "That's a fair amount." He scratched his head. "Let me guess, you need the money by April fourteenth?"

Angel nodded. "If it weren't for my sisters, I wouldn't even consider marrying a complete stranger but..."

"You feel responsible for them."

She sniffed, and moisture filled her eyes. "How can I not? I'm the oldest, and before my pa died, he told me to take care of Kitty and Teddy. It wasn't his fault he got behind on his mortgage payments. All the farms around here suffered from the grasshopper plague a couple of years back. The drought hasn't helped anyone either." She balled her hands in her lap. "I can't fail him—I won't fail him."

"Is that how you came up with the whole claptrap of finding a man? So, you can get your debts paid off?"

Essie's mouth went dry. When Judah said it like that, it made her sound like a villain. "I can't leave the home Pa worked so hard to make for all of us."

"What if your only way out is marrying that lout from Texas?" He grimaced.

Could she marry and move away from all she held dear? Live with a complete stranger—one who gave her a niggling of doubt concerning his honesty? Never see her sisters again. Tears welled up again and spilled down her cheeks.

She jumped up, crossing the room to busy herself with wiping crumbs from the dry sink. Hopefully, Judah hadn't noticed her tears.

Seconds later his hands settled on her shoulders, and she shrugged away from him as moisture continued to flow down her cheeks. No doubt her face had already turned blotchy. In her haste to put some distance between them, she stumbled over the braided rug.

Immediately his arms stopped her from falling. Caught off balance, her hands splayed across his chest as she struggled to stop her world from spinning. The Adam's apple in his neck bobbed as he swallowed and gazed down at her. Did she imagine it, or had his arms tightened around her back, drawing her closer to his body?

Her heart skittered. She'd never been so close to a man—except Pa. And when he'd held her, it hadn't been the same at all.

"Shhh, Angel." He patted her face, and his cheeks turned ruddy. "We'll find a way through this." He held her until her tears slowed.

His masculine scent filled her nostrils. She breathed deeply, resting her head against his chest. Content to stand in his arms and allow him to shield her from the world, even if it only lasted for the moment. She tipped her head back to thank him. His gaze held hers, and she didn't have a desire to move.

His head dipped, and his lips brushed hers. Tentative at first and then branding her mouth and heart in a way Timothy Miller never had.

Time stood still as his arms tightened around her again.

His lips caressed the top of her head, and he murmured against her hair, "Don't marry that milksop."

Her pulse quickened as his kisses blazed a trail down her neck.

"Marry me instead."

CHAPTER TEN

As the words left Jud's mouth, a gasp filtered into his consciousness. Kitty and Teddy stood in the doorway, their mouths gaping wide.

Angel shoved against his chest and out of his embrace, causing Jud to stumble backward. He didn't know what had come over him. He'd been so caught up in the illusion of having a fine woman in his arms. Living in a home with a family and loving every moment. Hadn't he resolved to himself that kind of normalcy wasn't for the likes of him? But he'd made that decision before they'd welcomed him into their home—before Angel took care of him.

"Oh, Essie, say yes." Kitty's eyes sparkled as she closed the door.

Angel's eyes glittered with leftover tears. "We don't even know who he is." She crossed the room and whipped out the newspaper he'd pulled from her bag earlier.

Jud cringed, waiting for the hangman's noose to tighten.

"If you ask me, he's a man worthy of your love." Kitty

winked at him and unbuttoned her coat.

Angel snorted. "Then why does he look like the wanted man in the paper?"

Her sisters crossed the distance and peered over Angel's shoulder. They all turned questioning glances his way.

Now he knew what a rabbit felt like when it caught sight of a pack of coyotes that had gotten a whiff of its scent. He swallowed and held up his hands. "I can explain."

"Your last name is Steele, isn't it?" Angel's chin lifted.

He closed his eyes for a fraction of a second and nodded. "There's an explanation—" His words were cut short as a sudden pounding on the door caused them all to jump.

"Who could that be?" Teddy muttered under her breath. "As if we don't have a barrel of pickles to deal with already." She crossed the room and flung the door open.

In stepped a tall man with a star pinned to his dark coat. Jud hung his head. *Why now?* Of all the times for the law to catch up with him, why did it have to be now?

The man surveyed the room, his gaze settling on Jud. His hand rested on the pistol strapped to his side. "You J. Steele?"

Jud refrained from running a finger between his collar and his throat. "I'm Jud Steele. If you're here about the wanted poster, it's my cousin Jesse you're after, not me."

Angel sucked in her breath, and her hand flew to her chest.

The lawman scrubbed his left hand across the stubble on his lower face. "A bounty hunter stopped by my office and said he shot Jesse in the leg about a month ago, but he got away before he could capture him. You wouldn't have a leg wound, would you?"

"That fella shot before even asking questions." Jud frowned. "He didn't give me a chance to explain."

"I'm sure you have the wrong man." Kitty stepped forward and placed a hand on Jud's arm. "You heard him. It's his cousin you want, not Judah."

Angel's lips pinched together, but she said not a word. He'd been willing to give his life savings to cover her debt and take her as his bride. To have a home with a good woman by his side. Apparently, his growing feelings for her were only one-sided. Jud sighed. He should have told her the truth sooner.

The lawman eased forward, one hand still on his gun. He withdrew a set of handcuffs with his other. "I'm going to need you to come with me, son, until we can get this straightened out."

Jud shuddered as the cold steel bracelets slipped around his wrists. His shoulders slumped as the lawman led him toward the door.

"Essie, say something." Kitty's eyes filled with tears. "He proposed, and you're going to let him go without a fight. What's the matter with you?" She grabbed his coat, wrapping it around his shoulders.

Teddy ran a hand across her face and wouldn't meet his eyes.

Jud glanced back one more time.

Angel stood with her head bent.

The thud of the door closing reverberated in his chest. His hopes of having a family again vanished like the puff of his breath on the cold air.

Essie's hopes of saving her sisters ran like water through her fingers as the lawman led Judah away. He hadn't been serious about his marriage proposal. No doubt the words had only slipped out before he'd had time to think about it.

That kiss. Her fingertips rested on her lips. Nothing like Timothy Miller's. She couldn't deny the way Judah stirred emotions in her she'd never experienced before. Had he felt it too?

"Essie?" Kitty's voice interrupted her thoughts. "Why didn't you fight for him?"

"You'd be a fool to think he's the man from the newspaper." Teddy stood with her feet planted, a fierce expression on her face. "I can't imagine what it's been like for Judah to be on the run 'cause of somethin' his cousin did. It's not his fault they look similar."

"And that kiss." Kitty covered her rosy cheeks with her hands. "It made me swoon seeing you two together in each other's arms. I hope someday I have a fellow interested in me the way Judah is in you."

"You really think he cares for me?" Essie studied her sisters' faces.

"How can you *not* see it?" Teddy snorted. "Some romance writer you are. You wouldn't know love if it came up and slapped you across the face."

Love? Judah had mentioned nothing about love. Essie had only wanted a marriage of convenience. She hadn't wanted to give her heart to another man. Especially not after Timothy Miller had crushed hers by canceling their engagement. All because of money. Or lack thereof.

No, she wouldn't consider marriage as a ploy to get the money she needed anymore. If she ever became a bride, it would be for love, not to save her family. "I have to tell you both something. You'd better sit down."

Her sisters exchanged glances before settling at the table and waiting for her to continue.

Essie took a seat across from them and drew in a deep breath. "Timothy changed his mind about marrying me when he found out how destitute we are."

Kitty leaned forward. "I never cared for Timothy. He didn't recognize something beautiful when he saw it."

"Things can't be that bad." Teddy shoved back her Stetson. "I know we haven't had good crops the past few years, but things are bound to be different come spring."

"I had hoped to save us by selling a story." Essie's shoulders drooped. "But I've only been able to write swill ever since Timothy..."

"Never mind about him. You're better off without him." Kitty grabbed her hand. "We can get through this together. You'll see."

Essie shook her head, and a tear spilled down her cheek. "You don't understand. We're going to lose our home. The farm. Everything Pa worked so hard to have for us."

"How? The bank can't do that, can it?"

"What were you thinkin' to not tellin' us sooner? Why?"

Her sisters fired questions so fast they took her breath away.

"If we don't come up with a hundred dollars by the fourteenth of April, the bank will take everything from us."

Teddy shoved to her feet. "They can't do that."

"I'm afraid they can. So, you see, we don't have many options." Essie hung her head.

"What are we going to do?" Panic lined Kitty's voice as she twisted her hands in her lap.

"What we should've done as soon as you found out about this, Essie." Teddy plopped back into the chair and reached for both of their hands. "We'll pray, askin' God to intervene. Only He knows what's best and has the answer for us. We need to trust Him."

Essie smarted at her youngest sister's words. Something she should've thought of and done on her own. "I'm sorry I didn't tell you both sooner."

"It don't do no good to keep secrets to yourself." Teddy wagged her head. "They just fester, like Judah's wound did. That's what got him in trouble too. He tried to keep his true identity hidden from us. Probably to protect us."

Essie heaved a sigh. "You're right, Teddy. Forgive me?"

"Of course, I forgive you." Teddy nodded toward the door. "But it's his forgiveness you should be asking."

"You never answered his proposal." Kitty scowled at her. "Teddy, saddle the horse so Essie can head to the jail and speak with Judah."

"No." Essie cleared her throat. "I will not marry the man so we can have our finances taken care of. I'm sure he didn't mean it and regrets it already."

"Did you get hit upside the head? The fella is head over heels in love with you." Teddy paced the small room.

"He didn't say that."

"Silly. He didn't have time to before the sheriff showed up. Go into town and give the man the opportunity." Kitty pierced Essie with a glare.

"You really think he cares for me?" She glanced at both of her sisters.

Teddy snorted. "He's been makin' moon eyes at you for the past couple weeks, and you've been makin' 'em right back at him."

Kitty fluttered her eyelashes. "It's been so romantic. I think if you allow yourself to study the matter, you'll realize that you have feelings for him, too."

While she couldn't deny a growing attraction to the cowboy, surely there were things that needed considering—like how to clear the man's name and get him out of jail.

CHAPTER ELEVEN

E ssie stood and arched her back. No story had ever flowed so easily. She hoped it was a good sign. *Thank You, Lord.* She scudded the papers together in an orderly pile, tied a piece of twine around them, and wrapped the story in brown paper with additional twine.

The mile between her home and town barely registered as she scurried to the post office before it closed for the day.

Hiram Brown smiled at her when he saw the package. "Looks like you've got another novel ready for a publisher?"

She nodded.

"I'll be praying they want this one."

"Thank you." She handed him money enough to cover the cost of the postage. When he handed her the change, she stared at the coins.

"Is there something the matter?" He leaned over the counter. "Did I count wrong?"

"Hmm? No. Oh, thank you, Mr. Brown. You gave me a wonderful idea." She didn't wait for his response but tore off down the street to the telegraph office.

She arrived with fifteen minutes to spare before the building shut down until the next morning. Stepping inside, she penciled her message and handed it to the clerk. He touched each word as he counted them and named a price to send the missive.

"I'd like to send that to every major city in the state." Essie loosened the string ties of her reticule.

"Whew. Never had a message gone out to so many folks at once." His thin cheeks tugged into a grin. "I'll let you know as soon as I get a response from someone."

"Thank you." She adjusted her hat. "Good day."

He didn't answer, already tapping out the message on his machine.

Her heart lightened as she closed the door behind her.

"Well, hello there, Miss Love." Benjamin Wilcox dipped his hat toward her. "Might I have the pleasure of your company for supper? Perhaps we can discuss our marriage plans. I've delayed leaving until I had your answer. Every time I tried to speak with you at your home, your sister chased me away."

She shook her head. "I'm afraid I won't be able to leave Kansas, Mr. Wilcox. My sisters need me, and I don't aim to disappoint them."

"Surely they are of an age where they can take care of themselves." A frown marred his features.

"That may be, but I still can't marry you."

His hand gripped her arm, preventing her from leaving. "It's because of the rabble-rouser who was visiting you. He's the cause of your change of heart, isn't he? I didn't think you wanted a cowboy."

Essie *hadn't* wanted a cowboy until God had dropped one into her lap—or at least onto her doorstep. Now she couldn't stop thinking about one Judah Steele. "Sometimes God gives us what we don't expect, but what we need the most." She moved away from the man's grasp. "Good day, Mr. Wilcox."

Jud shook the cell bars. Their rattling echoed back to him in the still room. Over three weeks had passed since the sheriff had arrested him for his cousin's crimes, but no matter what argument he gave, the lawman refused to release Jud. The man's continual answer was that he was checking into things, and waiting to hear back took time. Jud puffed out a deep breath and crossed to the tiny window and peered at the street. Snow had given way to green grass and flowers poking through on the thin branches of trees. Dropping back onto his bunk, he sprawled out on the worn mattress.

Angel hadn't come to see him. Not once.

A scuffing sound at the door to his cell drew his attention.

"You've got a visitor." The lawman glanced back toward the doorway. "If you behave, I'll let her into the cell with you."

Her? His heartbeat sped up. *Angel.* But when his gaze swung toward the woman approaching, disappointment coursed through his frame. Not Angel.

A smile flitted across Kitty's face as the lawman opened

the cell door, but she waited until he closed it behind her before she spoke. "I know you were expecting Essie, but she's been a little busy."

Too busy to visit? Probably thought his offer to marry her had been a grim joke. At first, the marriage proposal had been a way of taking care of her and her sisters. An honorable thing to do. If anything, during his stay in jail he'd come to the point of realizing what he wanted in life—he wanted Angel. Too bad she didn't care for him. He pasted on what he hoped served as a smile. "Howdy, Kitty. What can I do for you?"

She stared at him for a full minute before speaking again. "Don't give up on Essie. She's been coming by every day to see you. In fact, we all have." She nodded toward the door. "We haven't made it past that lout before now. I think I finally wore him down." Kitty batted her eyes and gave a coy smile.

A chuckle rippled from him. He couldn't remember the last time he'd laughed. His angel *hadn't* abandoned him after all. His chest eased.

Kitty's voice lowered. "I think he wouldn't let Essie in since he could tell you two are courting."

Courting? Did that mean she'd consider his proposal?

"Of course, the sheriff wouldn't let Teddy in since she usually came toting her gun and likely with an angry expression." Kitty's eyes twinkled. "Me, on the other hand, I've been trying to sweet-talk my way in here. I guess it finally worked."

Kitty hugged a brown-paper-wrapped package close to her chest. "Did Essie tell you she was engaged once?"

His head shot up. "She what?"

Kitty nodded. "Timothy Miller. He works at the bank in town."

That explained her dislike of bankers. At least one in particular. Maybe two.

"Honestly, I don't know if she even cared that much about him. I think he represented security for her...for us." She shifted the package in her arms. "When he discovered Pa left us with a note on the mortgage, Timothy decided he didn't want to marry Essie anymore."

Jud wasn't a violent man, but right then he wanted to slug Timothy Miller.

"Essie hasn't been able to sell a story since her broken engagement. It changed her and affected her writing." Kitty waggled her eyebrows. "She needed a handsome stranger to come along and shake things up in her world."

He didn't want to hear about Benjamin Wilcox and how the scoundrel was going to marry her and take her away to Texas. Especially when he was stuck behind bars and couldn't do anything about it.

"Essie's been doing whatever she can to pay off the debt we owe the bank. It's why she placed an advertisement in the paper, trying to get someone to marry her." Kitty flicked a piece of lint from her dress. "She's decided she will not wed just to save our home."

Air seeped out of his lungs. So, he didn't need to worry about Benjamin after all. That was the first good news he'd heard since being thrown in prison.

Kitty grinned at him. "In fact, Essie's determined not to get married..."

That was supposed to be *good* news?

"... at least not for the wrong reason. She wants to marry for love." Kitty's shoulders shook as she laughed. "You are a bit slow, aren't you?"

Wait. What had he missed?

She sighed. "I suppose I need to spell it out for you. She wants to marry *you*."

"She does?" His heart raced. "Angel never answered when I asked her."

"Well, if you remember, things were a little crazy that evening when the sheriff showed up." A smile tugged at Kitty's lips. "I'm sure *when* you ask her again, she'll say yes."

He paced back and forth across the confining space. "What if I never get out of here?"

"Essie's working on that too, around her other project." Kitty handed him the wrapped package. "Would you like to see part of what she's been working on?"

What he really wanted to see was *his* Angel. He took the parcel and tossed it onto the bed.

Kitty stamped her foot, giving him a cross look. "Sometimes I think men can be thickheaded." She picked up the packet and handed it to him again.

Jud untied the string and the brown wrappings fell away. He flipped over a stack of papers and stared down at the title written with broad strokes. *An Angel for the Cowboy* by E. Love. Curious, he started reading the first few lines.

Angel Love stumbled against an object mostly covered by the newly fallen snow. She shivered from the cold and bent in the pale moonlight to see what had caused her steps to falter. The face of the handsomest man she'd ever seen stared back at her. It almost took her breath away.

He ran his finger across the words. She'd written about *him*. About *them*.

Kitty chuckled. "I'll leave you to read the rest."

Chapter Twelve

E ssie's fingers shook as she accepted the two telegrams, then gave a coin to the rider and closed the door. The first one came from Beadle & Adams, the potential publisher for her new story.

RECEIVED AN ANGEL FOR THE COWBOY STOP
CONTRACT WILL FOLLOW IN POST STOP
ONE-HUNDRED-DOLLAR CHECK WILL BE SENT FORTHWITH STOP

She sank to her knees beside the kitchen chair. *Forgive me, Lord, for doubting You. Thank You for Your provisions. Please be with Judah. I pray, if it's in Your will, that You find a way to bring us together. In Jesus' name, amen.*

As she stood, the second envelope fluttered to the floor. She stooped to pick up the missive. Her heart skittered when she saw the return address. Kansas City, Kansas.

She'd sent telegrams to towns across the state to find more information on Jesse Steele. *Finally.* The first response had arrived. It had come from a nearby town marshal.

THANK YOU FOR YOUR RECENT INQUIRY STOP
JESSE STEELE INJURED IN TRAIN ROBBERY SIX MONTHS AGO STOP
MISSING LAST FINGER ON RIGHT HAND STOP
LAST SEEN IN CALIFORNIA STOP

A laugh bubbled on her lips, and she did a little jig around the kitchen. The door opened and shut behind her. She turned toward it.

"Essie?" Concern flickered across Teddy's face. "What happened?"

"The most wonderful news in all the world." She drew her youngest sister into her informal dance.

Teddy's mouth gaped open as she pulled them both to a halt.

"I need to borrow your horse. Is she still saddled?" Essie tucked both telegrams into her satchel and slung it over her shoulder.

"I don't know that I trust you to ride her when you're all befuddled." Teddy shook her head. "Maybe I should hitch up the wagon and take you wherever you need to go."

"I assure you, I'm better than I've been in a long while,

Teddy. Things are looking up. You wait and see." Essie hugged her sister and kissed her on the cheek. "I'll tell you all about it when I return."

She didn't wait for Teddy to respond. Instead, she tore out of the house to the barn, mounted, and urged the horse to a gallop.

The trip to town took far longer than she liked.

Finally, she brought Teddy's horse to a halt and dismounted. She flung the door of the sheriff's office open wide and stepped inside. "You're the man I want to see."

The sheriff glanced up in surprise. "Me? I've told you before I can't let you in to see the prisoner. You might sneak him a file or something."

Essie dug in her bag. "You need to read this telegram from the marshal in Kansas City. It arrived half an hour ago."

"Why would they be contacting you?"

She dipped her head. "Because I've been trying to find a better description of Jesse Steele."

"What makes you think he's not sitting in my cell back there?" He nodded toward the other room.

Essie jammed her hands on her hips. "The man I love is in your cell—*Judah* Steele, not Jesse." She poked her finger at the paper. "Read it."

"Women." The sheriff snatched the telegram from her outstretched hand. He skimmed the brief message. "Stay here." His tone brooked no argument.

She waited until he left and then crept after him, peeking around the doorframe.

"Hold up your hands, Steele."

"What?" Judah's voice sent delicious tremors down her spine.

"You heard me. Let me see your right hand. Might as well make it both of them." The sheriff moved close to the cell.

Essie poked her head around the doorframe so she could see, even though she knew the answer. She'd spent a month taking care of her cowboy.

"Well, I'll be. I guess the little lady knew what she was talking about." The lawman pulled a ring of keys from his belt. "It looks like you're free to go."

The click of the key in the lock was the sweetest sound she'd ever heard.

Jud smiled when he spotted Angel outside the jailhouse. He set her manuscript down, trotted to her, and swung her up and around in his arms. "I don't know how you did it or how I'll ever be able to thank you."

Her eyes sparkled as she laughed. "I can think of some ways. Now set me down so you don't hurt yourself."

He eased her to the ground and dropped a kiss on her forehead. "Is it true?" He picked up the wrapped package, patting it.

Her cheeks flamed. "An Angel for the Cowboy?"

He nodded. "Does the angel really care for the cowboy?"

"With all of her heart."

His heart thrummed in his chest. "Is it based on *my* angel?"

She didn't answer him immediately. "Most times a dime novel is purely fiction, but every once in a while, the story comes directly from a writer's heart."

He couldn't stop the grin from spreading across his face. He pulled her back into his arms and claimed her lips. She met him kiss for kiss, stirring his senses.

Jud couldn't tell how much time passed before he remembered they stood on the side of a very public street. He took a small step back, still holding onto her arms. "I'm sorry I didn't tell you sooner who I was, darling. I didn't want to do anything to risk losing you. Being with you and your sisters changed my life. I used to think I'd never be happy settling down and busting sod instead of riding the range, but if it means having a good woman like you, I'm all for it." He winked at her, dropping to one knee.

Angel's hand flew to her mouth.

He captured her other hand in his and heard the sharp intake of her breath.

Tears sparkled in her eyes. He hoped they were happy ones.

"Most would say that a gunshot wound is a bad thing, but to me it's been the best thing in my life." He drew her hand to his lips.

"It's changed my life as well." A shy smile shone on her face. "I'd become bitter, and it changed my writing...it changed me."

"Without my being shot, I would've never met you. Never have met the woman I've fallen in love with."

"You love me?"

"With all my heart, Angel. I'd be honored if you would

become my bride." He stood. "That is if you're willing to join ranks with a cowboy."

She threw her arms around his neck. "Oh yes. I thought you'd never ask."

He laughed. "I thought I'd be stuck in that jail cell the rest of my life."

"Not if I could help it."

"Speaking of helping, I plan to pay off what you owe the bank. Things will be tight at first, but I'm sure we'll work things out together."

She squeezed his arm. "I forgot to tell you. My story has already been accepted. They even sent a check in advance. Or at least it should be in the mail in the next few days or so."

He wrapped his arms around her, whirling her again. "That's wonderful, Angel. I'm so proud of you."

She beamed.

"I guess we don't have any reason to wait then. I hope you don't mind a spring wedding, darling, because I don't want to wait any longer to marry you."

EPILOGUE

April 14, 1876

Y ou may kiss the bride."

Jud's heart soared as he touched his lips to Essie's.

She pulled back a smidge. Her hand settled on the side of his face, and her cheeks flushed. "I have you to thank for all this. There wouldn't have been a story or a wedding without you."

"I'm happy to oblige, ma'am." He tipped his head toward her and snatched another smooch.

Angel giggled.

Kitty sighed, and whispered in a low voice, "I hope I can find a husband as wonderful as Judah."

Teddy snorted. "Not me. You won't ever catch me pinin' after a fella."

Judah ignored his two sisters-in-law and concentrated on his new wife. "I'm sure I can be the inspiration for a whole lot more of your stories, Angel."

He leaned in for another kiss, but his wife chuckled and

rolled her eyes. "I think I've created a monster."

"There's no chance of getting rid of me now, darling. You've already married me."

A dazzling smile shone across her face. "I guess there's no way around it then."

Jud savored another lengthy kiss. "Way around what?"

She nuzzled closer. "Who knew a cowboy and an angel would make such a good team?"

He drew her tight. "God did."

COURTING LOVE

PICKING A BRIDE FOR PAUL

I charge you, O daughters of Jerusalem, that ye stir not up, nor awake my love, until he please.

Song of Solomon 8:4 (KJV)

CHAPTER ONE

October 22, 1876,
Yoder Grove, Kansas

P oor Paul Baker."

Theodora Love jerked her head at her sister's comment. "What do you mean? Did somethin' happen to Paul?" A punch in the gut would've been less painful. Her heart pounded in her ears. *Not Paul, Lord. Help him with whatever's ailin' him.*

Kitty removed her hat, bedecked in ribbons and other such nonsense, patting her blonde hair before she turned to face Teddy.

Teddy sighed at her sister's dramatic pause. Why didn't she get on with it already?

Kitty frowned. "Didn't you hear at church this morning? He broke his leg two weeks ago."

"Two weeks!" Teddy gripped the back of a wooden chair. "How? Why didn't we hear anythin' sooner? We've been so busy with harvestin' I haven't had a chance to stop by."

"What's that?" Her oldest sister, Essie waddled into the kitchen with her husband, Jud Steele, trailing behind her.

Jud tugged a chair from beneath the kitchen table and kissed Essie's cheek. "Here, Angel, why don't you sit yourself down while your sisters and I rustle up some grub. You need to take care of that baby." He glanced at them. "What're you two talking about?"

Teddy wanted to shake her middle sister until she told her everything she knew about their neighbor's injury. "Kitty! What's wrong with Paul?"

"Hmm? Oh, yes, Doc Master's mother mentioned it after church. Said the poor man broke his leg right after he finished the harvest at his farm. Apparently, he's in a cast and is having a hard time taking care of things. I guess he's worried about getting his winter wheat planted, especially since most have already been sown." Kitty stripped her gloves from her fingers and tucked them inside her hat.

"How terrible." Essie's hand rested on her bulging stomach. "We need to find a way to help him."

"I can ride over there and offer my hand with the planting tomorrow." Jud shoved his hands into his pockets.

"If he needs assistance around the house, I can offer my services." Kitty tied an apron around her waist.

Teddy shook her head. "I can do all those things. Kitty, you're busy with takin' care of the needs here at home, especially with Essie increasin'. And Jud, if you see to finishin' off the plantin' here, I can go over to Paul's place and check what needs to be done. You've been farmin' enough now to know what we have to accomplish." Ever since he joined the family by marrying Essie back in April, he'd thrown himself into learning how to farm instead of riding the range.

Her sisters and brother-in-law stared at her like she had suddenly grown two heads. "What?" She put as much surprise in her voice as she could muster. "I'm not afraid to lend a hand."

"You've never assisted in the kitchen before." Kitty's blue eyes widened. "Are you sure you know what to do?"

"Of course, I do." *How hard can it be?* "Besides, he's my best friend." Teddy settled her Stetson in place and shrugged back into her coat. "I think I'll head there now so I get a better feel of what all it's goin' to take to get the job done."

"You haven't even had lunch yet." Kitty motioned toward the stove.

The scent of baked chicken wafted her way, causing Teddy's stomach to grumble in complaint. "Do you have enough to share with Paul?"

Kitty nodded. "I baked two chickens in case we invited someone home from church today. I'll get a basket ready while you saddle your horse."

Teddy secured the last button on her coat and reached for the door latch. Once outside, she breathed in the cool, crisp air. Her gaze settled on the fields where they'd recently harvested their corn. While she hadn't minded having Jud help with that task, sharing the maintenance of the farm with him chaffed like a sore on a hound dog. She missed being able to make decisions on her own.

She released her breath. *Don't get me wrong, Lord. I love Jud. He's the best man to take care of Essie, but the house is gettin' mighty crowded. And before too long, the baby will be here. What*

I wouldn't do for a place of my own where I can be in charge, or at least not be in the way.

Not that Essie or Jud had ever said such a thing, but seeing them with their heads together sharing a whispered conversation or hearing Essie giggling in the night made Teddy feel out of place. Like she needed to move on with her life. The question was—where could she move to that her sisters wouldn't put up a fuss and insist she stay with them?

Paul Baker hobbled across the kitchen floor and flung the door wide. The cool air did little to calm the storm within. He longed to be outside every day, working in the fields, taking care of his farm. Instead, he limped along like an old man. He hefted a sigh as he glared at the porch steps that kept him bound to the house. Last time he tried to climb down them, he fell face first in the dirt. Pain had seared through his broken limb.

He slumped into a chair on the porch and carefully lifted his leg onto a stool. The steady rhythm of a cantering horse drew his attention. Paul smiled as a rider on horseback rounded the bend in the road and came to a halt in front of the stoop. "Howdy, Teddy."

She swung down from her horse with natural grace. A frown marred her face and lines wrinkled her broad forehead. She lifted a basket from the saddle horn, clomped up the steps, and stared at his cast. "What did you do?"

He scrubbed a hand across the stubble covering his lower face. "The horse startled when I was getting down from the wagon seat. My foot caught on something, and I fell. The back wheel ran over my leg and broke it. Doc says I'll be in this cast until sometime in December." He tapped his knuckles against his encased leg.

She tilted her Stetson further back on her head, and her bright blue eyes studied him for a few seconds. "I brought lunch, and I'm here to help. Figured I can get your winter wheat in the ground and fix you meals and such. Whatever you need, I'm the gal to take care of it."

He couldn't help laughing. "You wouldn't know the first thing about finding your way around the kitchen. Kitty's done the cooking at your place since she was a young girl. Closest you got to cooking was eating." He couldn't keep a grin from spreading. "She'd be inside baking while you tagged along after me."

Teddy scowled and crossed her arms. "Never heard you complainin' none about me followin' you."

No. It'd always been nice to have her company. He welcomed it now too. "Don't get your britches in a knot. Just because Ma always said you ran as wild as a fox doesn't mean I wished you'd spent more time in the kitchen."

Her face sobered. "How's your ma doing? Have you heard from her since she moved to Texas to be with Miriam and her brood?"

He shook his head. "Not recently."

"Did you get word to her about what happened to you?"

"She'd only fret and want to come back." He ran a hand

along the tight muscles in his neck. "You know she hasn't been doing well since Pa died. I can't bear to ask her to come back to take care of me. She was heartbroken living here without Pa, and I won't ask her to do it again."

Teddy leaned against the pillar and crossed her legs. Her blue eyes twinkling. "You always were an *old* ornery thing."

He raised an eyebrow. "Who are you calling old? Five years isn't that big of a difference."

"You're practically an old man at twenty-four. I'm surprised the women haven't been flockin' around to help you though."

Would she care if they did? Paul shook off the thought. "I guess word hasn't made it through town yet." He shifted his leg. "How'd you hear about it?"

"Kitty heard somethin' at church this mornin' from Doc's ma. You know how that woman likes to gossip. Guess nothin' else interestin' happens for her to talk about." She shifted the basket on her arm. "Speakin' of Kitty, she sent some vittles."

"I hope you brought enough for both of us. I could use the company." He wobbled as he tried to stand and balance his crutches at the same time.

Teddy rushed forward and helped to steady him.

He smiled his thanks. "Still trying to learn how to use these confounded things."

"Kitty packed plenty of food. I'll set the table." She held the door for him and followed. Once they reached the kitchen, she pulled out a chair, and he settled into it. After making sure he was situated, she opened cupboard doors and retrieved plates and cutlery. Teddy poured them both a glass of water and then dished the food onto two plates.

He bent his head and said the prayer before stabbing a piece of chicken. "Mmm. Kitty sure knows how to cook."

"Speakin' of. Figured I could cook your meals until you're up on two feet again." She took a huge bite of a chicken leg and chewed. She glanced around the room. "Looks like you could use some help around the house too."

He huffed. "Yeah. I haven't been able to keep up with the place. I drop things and then I can't bend over and pick them up." He glanced at a stack of dirty dishes on the dry sink and items sprawled across the floor. "Maybe you could help clean the place and get it ready."

Her gaze snapped to meet his. "Get it ready for what?"

"My mail-order bride."

Chapter Two

A sharp pang shot through Teddy's chest. It made no sense for her body to react like that to Paul's comment. She cleared her throat. "Your who?"

"Mail-order bride. Before she left, Ma made me promise to find a wife. Figured sending for one was the easiest way to find one." He scraped his fork across his plate, scooping up every last dollop of mashed potatoes and gravy. "Ma didn't want me living here alone and suggested I send for a gal from the East."

"Oh? Any gal in particular?"

"No. I advertised about a month ago and have received a few letters so far. I'd like you to read through them and let me know what you think. It doesn't hurt to have a feminine perspective, especially from the one who knows me best." He waggled his eyebrows at her. "Maybe you can head into town tomorrow too and see if any more notes have come in since my accident."

"No problem, although I thought maybe first, you'd want

me to start on the plantin'." She shoved her plate away, unable to finish her last piece of chicken.

Paul's dark brown eyes studied her. "Are you feeling poorly? Never seen you pass up on eating all your food."

"Guess I'm just off my feed today." She nudged her plate closer to him. "Help yourself."

"If you're sure." He grabbed it before she had a chance to say otherwise. "I've been starving. You don't know how hard it is to balance on those things." He motioned toward his crutches. "And make a meal at the same time. Doc says I can't put any pressure on my leg. It was all I could do to persuade him to give me the crutches. He wanted me to be on bed rest until the bone healed."

"Must be rough. How have you been takin' care of your stock?"

"Doc arranged for one of the boys in town to come out twice a day and see to their needs. Wish he would've also asked someone to bring meals."

"There's no need to worry about that now. I'll make sure you're fed."

He rubbed his stomach. "That's what I'm afraid of."

She reached across the table and slugged his arm. "I tell you, cookin' can't be that hard. If I can sow a field of wheat, I can surely stir up a mess of hotcakes, fry bacon, or whip up potatoes."

Paul snorted. "Remember when Kitty tried to teach you to hem a dress?"

Teddy glared at him. "My big fingers weren't made for sewin' little tiny stitches."

He slapped his knee. "I still don't see how you ended

up stitching it to your pants and the tablecloth. Never saw something so funny as your face when you stood up and the dress and table covering came along with you." He guffawed.

"I was only eight. I've improved since then." He opened his mouth to say something, but she cut him off. "Where're the letters you mentioned? I'll fetch them for you."

Paul inclined his head in the direction of his bedroom. She stood and crossed the room, hesitating in the doorway.

"You can go in. Excuse the mess. You'll find them on the table beside the bed."

Teddy gathered her courage and stepped inside the room. In all her years playing at his place as a child, his ma had never allowed her to enter his bedroom. Teddy peeked over her shoulder as if to assure herself the woman wasn't there to reprimand her.

A pile of clothes lay in a corner of the room. He had toiletries spread across the top of a chest of drawers standing along one wall. The unmade bed took up most of the room. She hurried to the nightstand. A lantern, a Bible, and a small stack of letters covered the small piece of furniture. She scooped up the missives and retraced her steps.

Paul wiped his hands on a cloth napkin and then stood. "Let's go to the sitting room so I can get this blasted leg up. It pounds something fierce when I have it down."

"Don't you want me to take care of the dishes first?" She glanced at the dry sink. "Looks like you've about used up every plate, bowl, cup, and piece of cutlery your ma owned."

"No, I still haven't gone through her fancy dishes in the

cupboard in the sitting room." He waggled his eyebrows like he always had when he joked with her, and situated the crutches under his armpits.

She chuckled and followed him into the room, keeping an eye on his progress to make sure he didn't stumble. After he plopped onto a settee, she fluffed a pillow and set it on a hassock for him to rest his leg.

"Thank you." He wiped the sweat from his brow. "Would've never thought walking or hobbling could be so much work. Now, start reading the letters aloud so I can hear what you think of each one. As my closest friend, I value your opinion. Figured you might know a thing or two about what kind of wife would be the best fit for me. I need your help picking one."

Paul watched as Teddy's lips pinched together like she'd bitten into a sour pickle. "Something bothering you?" He shifted his leg on the pillow. "Maybe you really are off your feed. Your face doesn't look so good."

She flipped the long, thick braid of brown hair behind her shoulder, her eyes snapping at him. "There isn't anythin' wrong with me." She snagged the letter on top and tore it from the envelope. "I don't rightly see why you want me to read it out loud to you. It's not like you haven't read them before." She glared at him.

He had no earthly idea what he'd done to stir up her anger. Fortunately, she didn't seem to need a response as she glanced back at the letter.

"Dear Paul. I live at home with my parents and my two cats." She stopped and poked her finger at the piece of paper. "You won't want this woman. If she mentions her cats, it means she'll want to bring them along. More than likely she's an old maid who can't find anyone to marry where she lives and is havin' to widen her search. Sounds desperate to me. Besides, she shouldn't be usin' your first name on account of not even meetin' you yet. If I were you, I wouldn't bother with her."

Teddy flicked the letter onto the arm of the chair beside her, not bothering to put it back in the envelope. She snatched up the next one in the stack and perused the note before she started reading it aloud.

"Dear Mr. Baker. I've had a longin' to see the West for several years now." Teddy flipped the letter to join the other one beside her. "Nope, she's no good either. The woman is only usin' you to get out here so she can do as she pleases. She's not reliable."

His head spun as Teddy worked her way through the five letters, only reading a few sentences of each before she found some reason to reject all the women as a potential wife for him. This was going to be harder than he had imagined. Two of the five letters he'd thought had been excellent prospects, but Teddy knew him best, and he trusted her.

She dusted her hands off. "Well, that was easy. There isn't a suitable match among them. But don't you worry, Paul. I will find the right bride for you."

He couldn't help but wonder what such a bride would

look like. What would it take to meet Teddy's approval?

Teddy collected the letters and carried them to the kitchen table. She'd like to throw them in the pile of trash to be burned, but she wouldn't until Paul gave her the go-ahead. Instead, she busied herself with boiling water, pouring it into a basin, and then adding soap chips. She stirred the water with a rag until suds appeared in the pan. A bubble escaped the steamy water and floated near her face. She popped it before she dunked a stack of dirty dishes in to soak.

What traits would a woman find irresistible about Paul? He was a hard worker and owned his farm. His muscular build and tall height showed how good he was at keeping up with the work.

She scrunched her nose and ticked each virtue off by raising a finger as she listed them. Paul was a godly man with a good sense of humor.

Kitty had mentioned once that their neighbor was good looking with his black hair and its slight wave, and his deep brown eyes. She'd shared that women found those features irresistible.

Hmmm. Funny, that had never affected Teddy.

The pile of clean dishes grew as she worked. The glasses sparkled as she set the last one in the cupboard and closed the door. She took the pan of dirty dishwater and flung it outside on the flowers planted along the porch.

Paul's mother had always insisted on being surrounded by beautiful things.

Teddy bit back a snort. Probably why his ma had never been too keen about Paul's close friendship with her. She certainly didn't measure up to the refined woman his ma was.

She ran her hand along the clean dry sink. What would it be like to have her own household and farm to take care of?

CHAPTER THREE

After almost a week and a half of reading together through the letters that came, Paul was about ready to give up on the whole mail-order bride idea. In fact, he would've, if he hadn't promised Ma to keep searching for a wife. The usually easy-to-please Teddy had found fault with every single prospect. He was beginning to wonder just how objective she was.

The sound of a horse snorting drew his attention away from his thoughts. He crossed to the window and lifted the blue gingham curtain. Doc Master swung down from the saddle and reached for his medical bag. Paul let the fabric fall back in place and opened the door. "Howdy, Doc."

The middle-aged man shoved his spectacles back up his nose. "Hello there, Paul. How are you and the leg faring?"

"Can't complain." He closed the door behind them. "Coffee is on the back of the stove if you'd like a cup."

Doc chuckled and made his way there. "Guess you still aren't up to carrying a mug with those things, are you?" He motioned to the crutches.

Paul released a sigh. "Tried to the other day, and I about scalded myself in the process."

"I thought Teddy Love was coming out to help you. Did she get angry and stop coming?"

His head swung up. "Why would you think that?"

"On account of you trying to find a bride."

"What does that have to do with anything?"

"My mother and I always figured you two would get hitched one day. Any fool could see you're like peas in a pod." His wrinkled cheeks tugged as he smiled. "I don't think I ever saw you without her following when you were growing up. She hasn't been too far away either since you've gotten older."

Paul didn't know how to respond.

"Brought your mail. Looks like you got another stack of letters from potential women. The whole town is abuzz about you sending for a mail-order bride."

"Guess it's a good thing I can't make it into town just yet. Otherwise, I'd get hammered with questions."

"You're right about that." Doc scratched his balding head. "Mother would likely be the one leading the charge to find out more."

Paul couldn't stop grinning even if he tried. Doc's ma was known for digging out information from folks.

"Let's see about that leg now." The man guzzled his last swallow of coffee and set the mug on the table.

A few minutes later, Doc snapped his medical bag shut and tugged the door open. "You're healing nicely. I set another packet of medicine for the pain on the table there if you need it. The pain should start slacking off soon and not bother you as much. If it doesn't subside by the next time I stop by, you'll have to stay off your feet completely and remain in bed until it fully heals, so don't overdo it. Got it?"

Paul nodded and followed the doc outside onto the porch. "I don't want that to happen. I've got too many things that need doing with a bride coming."

Doc peered at him over his glasses. "I guess you've given up on the idea of marrying Teddy then?" He secured his bag on the saddle horn and swung up onto his horse. "I hope you find the woman you're searching for. See you next week. If you need me before then, send word with one of the boys taking care of your animals."

Paul waved as the doc left, but he couldn't forget the man's words concerning Teddy. A memory from five years prior washed across his mind. He'd been the age Teddy was now, and she'd been fourteen. Her body had gone through changes that summer, and it was the first time he'd noticed her as more than just the little girl next door. Ma had sensed his growing attraction and stamped it out quick-like, stating Teddy was fine as a playmate, but she wasn't future wife material for him. Ma'd insisted he look for someone who had refined manners and was genteel. Two qualities that his next-door neighbor would never have.

He shoved the thought aside. Teddy wouldn't consider him as a potential husband, so it was no use even pondering it. He reached for the stack of letters, ripped one open, and started reading.

His pulse increased as he reread the letter. This gal had

potential and all the qualities Ma had told him to look for. He wouldn't wait for Teddy's opinion. *No.* More than likely she'd find something to criticize if she read the missive. Decision made, he stood and hobbled into the sitting room to the small desk in the corner. He sank into the straight-backed chair and uncapped the ink bottle and started writing a response.

Teddy held her breath as she opened the door to the cookstove, praying the cake would turn out this time. Her last three attempts had ended up in the pig trough. If this one didn't work, she'd have to scrap the whole idea and get on over to Paul's place. He probably wondered what had happened to her. It was hours later than she normally arrived.

Kitty peered over her shoulder. "It smells and looks good this time."

Essie glanced up from her writing. "It's torture to keep smelling something baking and not get a chance to eat it. Are you planning on sharing any of it with us?"

"Not if it's a success. Paul hasn't had dessert in a while, and you know the sweet tooth he has." Teddy snatched a towel and lifted the pan from the oven.

Kitty hovered close as Teddy lightly touched the cake with a fork. It sprang back and didn't fall.

Her middle sister squeezed her arm. "I'm so excited for you." Her face beamed. "Did you want help icing it?"

She shook her head. "I want it to be somethin' I did on my own."

"You know, for as astute as you usually are, you seem to be blind when it comes to Paul." Essie used the table to push herself to standing and waddled closer.

"What d'ya mean?"

Her oldest sister rested her arm on her swollen belly as if it were a shelf to put things on. "You care for Paul."

"Well, of course I do. That's why I'm goin' there every day. Don't know what that has to do with bein' astute." Teddy stirred the vanilla frosting with a knife, plunged her pinky into it, and then popped her finger into her mouth. Sugary sweetness assaulted her taste buds. Perfect.

Essie and Kitty exchanged a look. She ignored her sisters and started spreading the frosting on the cake.

"You might want to let it cool before you do that." Kitty hovered at Teddy's arm. "Otherwise, it'll melt and be messy."

"There's no time. I'm already late gettin' to Paul's." She continued to cover the dessert with the gooey icing.

"You're avoiding me." Essie shoved closer.

"Just tryin' to get this finished without you two hoverin' and givin' pointers." She frowned at her sisters. Why couldn't they leave her be?

Essie snagged Teddy's hand. "Will you stop and listen for a minute? You keep avoiding what I'm trying to tell you, and I need to say something before it's too late."

"What're you talkin' about? Somethin' wrong with you or the baby?" Teddy's gaze dropped to her sister's belly.

Essie tugged her away from the cake.

Kitty followed.

"It's clear as anything to all of us, but you don't seem to see or recognize that you're in love with Paul. I'm guessing you have been for a long time, but you haven't wanted to say anything. If you don't tell him, he'll send for a bride, and you'll miss your chance to find happiness with him." Her oldest sister squeezed Teddy's hand.

She tugged free of Essie's grip. "You don't know what you're talkin' about."

"Don't I?" Essie's eyebrow lifted, and she gave Teddy a look that only a big sister can give.

"Can you really deny that you care for him?" Kitty chimed in.

Essie hedged closer. "Can you honestly tell us it doesn't matter to you if he sends for a wife and marries a stranger? His getting wed will mean you can't go traipsing over there whenever you feel like it and hang out with him in the barn or the fields." Something flickered in Essie's eyes.

"W-what do you mean? Why couldn't I?"

"Silly." Kitty gripped her shoulder. "No woman wants to share her man with another woman."

"Why not?" Teddy planted her hands on her fist and glared at her sisters. The two gazed back and forth at each other as if they knew something that she didn't. "What?"

Kitty threaded her arm through Teddy's and squeezed her waist.

"Let me put it this way. How would it be if Mary Beth White from town always came here and wanted to spend time with Jud?" Essie inched closer to Teddy.

"Why, that's plain silly. You wouldn't want her

monopolizin' ..." Ice trickled up Teddy's spine.

Paul's getting married would change everything. She'd no longer have someone to go to when her sisters drove her crazy, or when she needed advice, or when she just wanted to spend time with him because she enjoyed his company. Teddy swallowed past the rock digging in her throat.

His getting a bride meant the end of a lifelong friendship. Why hadn't she seen it sooner? Was it too late to do something about it?

Chapter Four

T eddy dismounted from the wagon seat, shaking her skirt to fall in place around her boots. She reached for the cake when a whistle rang out from the porch.

"Is that really you, Teddy?" The thud of Paul's crutches thwacked against the wooden boards.

She turned to face him, her head already aching from the pins stabbing into the weight of her braided hair, which Kitty had secured before Teddy had left home. She didn't know how her sisters dealt with having their hair up and wearing confounded dresses every day. It was enough to drive a gal to distraction.

"Teddy?" Paul's voice snagged her from her woolgathering. "Why are you all spiffed up? Did someone die? I haven't seen you wear a dress since you were maybe five years old, except for your pa's funeral."

She swallowed and lifted the skirt a smidgen so she wouldn't trip over the hem. "Nobody died. Just figured it wouldn't hurt for me to dress like a woman every once in a while."

He stared at her slack-jawed, his gaze traveling up and down as he studied her. A smile finally lit his face. "You look downright pretty. I don't think I've ever seen you with your hair up. It makes you seem older."

Did he like it? Or should she have never listened to her sisters when they came up with the idea of how she could woo their neighbor. Fiddlesticks. She should've put her foot down and stopped their nonsense.

"I like it." His grin shot wide. "You know, if you dress like that more often and put your hair up, you'll likely snag the attention of one of the fellas in town. Although I like your hair down. You're always talking about wanting a place of your own. If you keep dressing like that, you'll be married in no time. Then we'll both have what we want."

She froze for a second. His words were like tiny ice pellets piercing her heart.

"What's that you got there?" He licked his lips.

"A cake."

He rubbed his stomach. "Mmm. Kitty's been baking, huh? It looks like my favorite."

She clamored up the steps and carried the plate inside, placing it on the table with a thunk. He thumped behind her. Teddy turned, thrusting her hands onto her hips. "*I* made it."

"*You?* I know your cooking is getting a little better, but I didn't think you knew how to bake."

She didn't meet his gaze. "I, uh, I asked Kitty to teach me."

His brow puckered. "Since when did you develop an interest in domestic tasks? You've done a fine job here getting the place cleaned up and keeping me fed, but I know you're more comfortable out in the fields or working with the animals in the barn. Why the sudden change? And I don't for one minute believe your reason for why you're all gussied up."

"A gal doesn't have to tell a fella everything, you know." She tugged open a drawer and removed a knife before slamming it shut. Teddy set the utensil down with a thud.

Confusion splashed across Paul's face. "There's no reason to get all testy. What's wrong with you? You're acting all female all of a sudden."

She jammed her fists on her waist again. "And what's wrong with that?" The knot in her gut cinched tighter.

"Nothing when it's one of your sisters, but I expect you to be different. You always have been. I suppose that's why we've gotten along so well through the years."

He was right. She'd turned into a green-eyed woman snarling as if she had a swarm of bees in her bonnet, all because of her sisters. What did they know? She should be able to persuade him to stop looking for a bride and consider her instead. After all, he was reasonable. Most men were. It was women who had trouble talking out their differences and got all weepy-eyed in the process.

"You're right. Guess I'm like a mutt covered in fleas today. All scratch and no comfort. Sorry about that. Forgive me?" She reached her hand toward him.

He stared at it for a moment, then shook it.

With a nod, she pulled out his chair and waited until he sat before she placed a huge slice of cake in front of him. She cut a generous piece for herself and then sank into a chair across from him.

He studied the cake for a moment, eyes narrowed. She couldn't help examining it too. Her sisters had been right. The icing had melted, so the cake didn't look very good. But it smelled delicious. Paul cut off a tiny bite, popping it in his mouth.

She tapped her foot as she waited for his thoughts about it.

Paul's eyes closed. "Mmm. This is delicious, Teddy. You've outdone yourself." He opened his eyes and grinned.

She returned his smile.

"Maybe you can make this cake for my wedding."

Her fork hit the wooden table with a clatter.

He withdrew an envelope from his shirt pocket. "Finally took the plunge. Found a woman I'm interested in, and I'm sending for her to come right away. Figured it's best if we got to know each other face-to-face. I was hoping you'd take the letter to town on your way home."

If Paul didn't know Teddy better, he'd say she had paled when he'd mentioned finding the mail-order bride he intended to marry. It made little sense though, since she'd shown no romantic interest in him in all their years of knowing each other. If she had, he would've done whatever it took to woo her and make her his.

She had him all discombobulated because she wore a dress and put her hair up today. No wonder the book of the

Song of Solomon in the Bible talked about not awakening love until the appropriate time. It made a man think strange thoughts. "Do you have clothes you can change into?"

This time, her face paled. "What?"

He motioned with his hand. "A man can't think straight when you're dressed like that."

A grin sprouted on her face, and her eyes twinkled. Confounded woman. If he didn't know better, he'd say she toyed with him like a cat playing with a mouse before he ate it. "The least you can do is take your hair down. Those pins must be pricking you something fierce."

"You said you like my hair down, didn't you?"

"Yes. I mean, that's pretty too." He motioned toward her head. "Don't know why you'd want to go and change things. You make a fella get a funny feeling in his gut when you have your hair up like that. Do you need help to take the pins out?"

"No. They're just fine where they are."

He frowned. Now she was being just plain ornery. He shoveled the last bit of cake into his mouth and cleared his throat.

She grabbed his plate and stood. "I had best get these taken care of and start on the meal."

"Don't worry about fixing one today. I still have some leftovers from the stew you made yesterday. I found a way to get down the steps and placed it in the root cellar so it would stay cold." He glanced out the window. "Well, will you look at that? It's starting to snow."

Teddy walked to the door and flung it open, letting in a blast of cold air. She stepped outside, and he followed her, closing the door. He watched as she traipsed down the steps and twirled around in a circle with her arms flung wide. Her skirt swirled around her heels, and she stuck out her tongue, trying to catch a snowflake. Something they always did as kids when they got the first snowfall of the season. They'd make it a game to see who tasted the first flake.

He allowed his armpits to rest on the top of each crutch as he watched her continue to twirl and laugh. How he wished he could join her without worrying about having his crutches slipping and sliding on the cold ground.

The heavy snow fell, quickly covering the ground in a blanket of white. Finally, Teddy joined him on the porch. The moisture from the snowflakes glistened on her eyelashes and lips, dusting her hair. He forced himself to glance away. A man had no business sending for a bride when he wanted to woo the one in front of him. He shoved his desire away.

"Isn't it glorious? I love snow."

"Me too. Let me get that letter, and you probably should be getting on your way." He glanced at the sky before he headed inside, holding the door open until she'd gotten over the threshold. Paul wobbled as he shut the door before righting himself and heading to the table.

His fingers fumbled with the envelope, and he dropped it on the floor.

Teddy bent, scooped it up, and tapped it against her knuckles. "Are you sure you want to send this?"

Right now, he wasn't sure of anything.

Teddy wished Essie or Kitty were here right now and could tell her what to do. The last thing she wanted was to take Paul's letter into town and mail it—to be a part of losing her best friend. She massaged the tight muscles in her temples where a headache was beginning to form.

She could've sworn she'd seen something in his face after joining him on the porch. Her sisters would've been able to interpret his expression, but not her.

Her chest constricted. Teddy wanted to crumple the letter he'd written to another woman. Instead, she shrugged into her coat, not bothering to secure the buttons. "I guess I'd best be goin'. Can't promise you when I'll get to town."

She left before he had a chance to respond, hoping he'd follow her to the porch and stop her.

He didn't.

CHAPTER FIVE

I don't know what to do." Teddy paced the confines of the small bedroom she shared with Kitty.

"You *have* to mail the letter. He'll figure something's up if he never hears a response from the woman. What's her name?" Kitty sat with her feet pulled up beneath her nightgown.

Teddy crossed the room and lifted the letter from their shared dresser, although she didn't need to. The name was already seared into her brain. "Catherine McDougal from New York." She plopped onto the end of the bed and kicked off her boots.

"It's a pretty name."

She scowled at her sister. "You should've told me long before now about my interest in Paul. I would've had a chance if I'd learned of it before he got this nonsense in his head about sendin' for a mail-order bride."

Giggles rumbled from Kitty. "That's pretty bad if you couldn't recognize it yourself and that you care for the man."

Teddy stripped down to her long handles, crawled under the covers, and stared at the ceiling. "I'm not like you. Besides, if you remember, we had to tell Essie about her lovin' Jud before she deciphered it. If you're like the rest of us Love sisters, you won't be able to tell either when the time comes."

"Oh, I don't know about that. I'm pretty sure I'll realize when I fall in love with a man well before you and Essie have." Kitty lowered her voice to a whisper. "Although sometimes I wonder if it'll ever happen."

"I kind of wish it hadn't happened to me." Teddy rolled to her side, propped her head on her hand, and studied her sister. "I think I was better off not knowin' than knowin'."

"You poor thing." Kitty leaned over and hugged her. "I think it's high time we pray about it together, don't you think?"

Teddy nodded and bowed her head. Her heart calmed as her sister prayed for her and Paul. She sent up a prayer of her own. *Lord, my life is Yours. If Paul is to be part of it, then I ask You to make a way for us, and if he isn't, then help me to accept that too.*

Kitty yawned and blew out the lamp. "Good night, Teddy."

"G'night." She snuggled under the covers, comforted in the fact that no matter what happened, she could trust God with the details.

November 23, 1876

Paul slicked down his hair and checked his reflection in the mirror one last time. A knock interrupted his primping. "Come in."

The door creaked open, and Teddy poked her head inside. "You decent?"

"I'll let you be the judge of that." He wiped his sweaty hands against the side of his pants.

"You look fair to middlin'." Her smile didn't register in her dark blue eyes. "Did you tell your mail-order bride that you're in a cast?"

"No. There really wasn't time. After I sent the letter and money for her to come, I only received one response in return saying she'd gotten the train ticket and should arrive today. I can't believe it's been three weeks."

Teddy nodded but didn't meet his gaze. She stood fiddling with her Stetson. "Maybe you should've found someone else to take you to the train station to meet her."

"Why? You're the only person I can think of to have there. I'm eager for Catherine to meet my best friend. Did you have somewhere you had to be today? I'm not keeping you from something, am I?"

She shrugged. "What time is she gettin' in?"

"12:15 if the train is on schedule. Thought maybe the three of us could go to lunch together afterward, and you could act as a chaperone. At least, until I get to know her better."

A stricken expression flickered across Teddy's face before she put her hat on, pulling it low so he couldn't read her thoughts in her eyes.

"Not sure I'll be available to be doin' much chaperonin'. Besides, you're an adult, and I've got things I need to see to."

"Like what?" He shrugged into his suit coat and adjusted the string tie that suddenly felt like it was constricting him.

"Need to check on the winter wheat."

He chuckled. "Sounds like an excuse to me. You know there's nothing to do with it until next summer. If I didn't know you better, I'd think you're wanting to avoid me. You've been using lame explanations for the past three weeks about why you couldn't be here. I've seen more of Jud than I have of you."

"I told you. We had some sick critters that needed tendin' to. Had to keep an eye out so we don't have other ones gettin' ill too." She scraped the toe of her boot along the floorboard, keeping her head down and not meeting his gaze.

"Don't know why Jud can't see to them instead of you." The crutches skitched as he reached for his hat. He caught his balance just in time. "I'll be so glad to be rid of these things."

"When did Doc say he'll remove the cast?"

"A little over a week from now. He wanted to make good and sure the bone was set before he took it off." He patted the pocket of his suit coat to make sure he'd put his wallet there. "I think I'm ready to go."

"I know you're tryin' to look all fancy for your, uh, bride, but you'll want to wear a coat." Teddy folded her arms across her chest. "We're not leavin' until you do. It's bitterly cold out there. Don't remember it ever bein' this cold so early in the season."

"You trying to be my ma?" He grinned at her before he hobbled over to the set of hooks on the wall beside the door and pulled on his coat. "Satisfied?"

Teddy grunted as she held the door open for him. She stayed beside him as he made his way down the few stairs and to the back of the wagon. He turned his back toward it and sat down, using his arms to skootch onto the pile of blankets she'd kept there to help cushion the ride for him whenever he had to get to town. Once he was situated, she secured the latch and laid the crutches beside him.

Neither of them spoke during the quick trip to Yoder Grove. Riding with his back toward her didn't make it conducive for conversation, not that he had an interest in talking. His brain kept bobbing like an apple in a pail of water as he worried over what Catherine would think of him.

He hunched deeper into his coat and blew on his hands, wishing he'd remembered to wear gloves. Little clouds puffed as he breathed in the cold air.

By the time they reached town, the shrill of the train whistle alerted him to its progress. His potential wife would be here in a matter of minutes. He tapped his fingers against his knee as Teddy parked the wagon by the station and secured the horses. Once she opened the tailgate, he slid to the edge, waiting for her to hand him his crutches.

Several folks lined the outside of the depot. He veered past them, nodding a greeting but not lingering to converse. Teddy pointed to a bench at the end of the walkway, and he headed toward it.

The train gave another brief toot, and he awkwardly paced a short distance, gripping his crutches.

"It would do you good to sit while you can." Teddy leaned against the wall of the station with her arms crossed, watching him.

He shook his head. "I don't think I could even if I wanted to." He blew out a tight breath. *Have I done the right thing, Lord? I'm thankful that You gave me the idea of a trial period to get to know each other first. I don't think I could've married her as soon as she stepped off the train. Don't know how folks do that. If Catherine isn't the woman You have for me, can You make it clear to both of us? I want to have a good marriage like my parents did. Someone who can work beside me, who will love me and the farm.* Someone like Teddy. He squelched the thought with a small jiggle of his noggin.

Paul forced his gaze to the tracks. The train came around the bend and soon screeched to a halt in front of him. His heart stampeded as the passenger door slid open, and the conductor jumped onto the platform before placing a stool on the ground. The man turned back toward the opening and reached his hand to assist a tall woman with black hair.

Her elaborate hat stood a good foot above her head and tilted to the side like it was about to slip off. Her gown was an ornate thing with a section of it trailing behind her as she started down the steps. She glanced his way, and her eyebrow lifted when Teddy came to join him. With a tiny head shake, she shifted her gaze to the other folks lining the walkway.

"You think that's Catherine?" Teddy's voice tickled his ear. "Never seen such a getup. Your ma probably would like her."

Ma might. *He* wasn't so sure.

CHAPTER SIX

T eddy gawked at the fancy woman who stepped off the train like a queen appearing before her subjects, kind of like the story Essie used to read to her younger sisters when they were little. The one that Kitty had oohed and aahed over and Teddy had thought was downright loco.

Paul appeared dumbstruck and hadn't made a move toward his mail-order bride. Teddy refused to be the first one to greet her, even if she already told the Lord that she'd accept the woman who'd be taking her place as Paul's best friend. She'd do best to remind herself that she was only here to be a driver and chaperone. Two tasks she would perform for him for a few days before she found someone else to take over the job. Someone who didn't have an inkling for Paul like she did.

The woman's deep blue dress didn't have a single wrinkle on it, or else the material hid them well. She turned sideways, and Teddy saw a hump on the lady's backside. What had Essie called those contraptions? Bustles. They were rare to see in Yoder Grove. More so when a traveler was passing through from a big city. Folks here on the prairie weren't as concerned about recent fashions, although Kitty did enjoy pouring over the latest lady's magazine whenever one came in the mail.

Finally, Paul started hobbling toward the woman.

Teddy trekked after him, stopping a few steps away, giving them time to meet.

Paul reached out and offered his hand to the lady.

The woman glanced at it as if unsure what to do next.

He cleared his throat and let his hand fall slack to his side. "Miss McDougal? Catherine? I'm Paul Baker." He reached back and snagged Teddy's arm, pulling her beside him. "I'd like you to meet my best friend, Teddy Love."

Catherine stared back and forth between the two of them for a few seconds before curtsying. "How do you do? I must say, I've never heard of a woman named Teddy before."

"Actually, it's short for Theodora. My pa was hopin' for sons." She dipped her hat toward the newcomer. "Pleased to meet you, Miss."

"Likewise." Catherine's gaze swung back toward Paul. "You didn't tell me about your injury."

"I didn't have time to. Broke my leg near the beginning of October, but I'll soon be without this cast." He tapped his knuckles against the plaster. "No need to worry about that."

"I see." Catherine's brow furrowed. "I must find someone who can tend my baggage."

"If you point it out, miss, I'll make sure it's loaded onto my wagon." Teddy watched as the railmen unloaded one of the train cars.

"It's that cluster of three trunks. Those with the brown buckles." Catherine pointed to a matched set.

"I'm sorry I can't help you, Teddy." Regret flashed across Paul's face.

"No need to worry." She backed away from the couple, thankful for the short reprieve.

A moment later she shouldered the largest of the three cases and strolled toward the wagon. Paul would be a might crowded with the luggage until they dropped Catherine off at the local boarding house. *Lord, help me be kind and not jealous of a woman I don't even know. Paul's ma would take a shine to her seein' as they both come from the east. I'm sure he will too since she's such a pretty thing.* Her chest tightened at the thought. Pretty hadn't ever been a word used to describe Teddy.

Shoving the thought aside, she hefted the case into the bed of the wagon and turned back for the other two. By the time she finished, she'd worked up a sweat despite the cold temperatures. Teddy swiped her forehead with her glove and set her Stetson back in place as she meandered toward the couple.

"Thank you." Catherine's face creased with a small smile as she threaded her fingers through the crook in Paul's arm. "Paul mentioned lunch at the local diner, and I understand you'll be joining us?" She removed her hand as he shifted the crutches and started heading toward the wagon.

Teddy dipped her head. "Wagon's over this way, miss."

"Please call me Catherine. Since you're such a good friend of Paul's, I hope we'll be able to become close as well."

"Never had a female friend before other than my sisters,

but they don't count."

Paul grinned as the two of them spoke. She couldn't tell what had tickled his funny bone, but he sure seemed pleased about something. Probably Catherine.

Teddy shook her musings aside like Kitty shaking out a dust cloth.

She'd work on being this woman's friend no matter how much it hurt to see Paul with someone other than herself. Sometimes being a good chum meant doing what was best for the other person, even when it caused a sharp stab to her chest.

Paul didn't know what to think of Catherine McDougal. She was a little too sophisticated for his liking, but he needed to keep an open mind. Honestly, he didn't see why Ma thought it was a necessary trait. It wasn't like he lived in the city where he had to know which fork to use at a fancy dinner or anything. He preferred the simple life he had on the farm. Would Catherine? Paul couldn't picture her milking a cow, planting a garden, or helping to slaughter pigs with her fancy getup.

He glanced at Teddy but couldn't tell what she was thinking as she helped him into the wagon. Paul sat sideways this time, resting his back against the side of the wagon so he'd be able to see the two women as they traveled the short distance to the local eatery. Catherine stood off to the side, beside the wagon, looking unsure what to do.

"You can hop on up onto the seat there." Teddy motioned to her. "I'll be 'round lickety-split."

Catherine lifted her skirt a smidge as she stared at the wheel and then the high seat. "I'm not sure how to do so. I've only ridden in buggies before, and I've always had someone assist me."

Teddy handed the crutches to him to hold since there wasn't any room beside him.

"Well, if you put your foot there." Teddy gestured to a spoke. "I can shove you up from behind, although I'm not sure if I'll hurt that contraption or not on your, uh…"

Paul bit the inside of his cheek to halt the snort of laughter that longed to break free.

"Oomph." Teddy vaulted Catherine toward the seat. "You're heavier than you look."

Catherine didn't respond, but her cheeks blazed with color.

He bit back a laugh.

Teddy dusted her hands off and jumped onto the seat, beside Catherine. She released the brake and clicked to the horses. "Normally we'd walk to the diner since it isn't far, but Paul hasn't been able to walk much of a distance on those crutches."

Catherine nodded but didn't reply. He couldn't help wondering what she thought of his little town. He imagined it was far different from New York.

A few minutes later, they sat at a small table in a corner of the dining area.

"I can leave so the two of you can have some alone time to talk while I sit over there." Teddy pointed to a table on the other side of the room.

He grabbed her hand. "No, stay with us. You don't mind, do you, Catherine?"

A smile lit her violet eyes. "Not at all, I'd love for you to eat with us, Teddy. Maybe you can tell me more about you and your sisters."

Teddy took a swallow of her coffee and then wiped her mouth with her hand. "Not much to tell. Essie's my oldest sister. She's married to Jud, and they'll be expectin' a little one before too long. She writes dime novels."

Teddy sold herself short. There were many fascinating things that could be told about her. Paul forced himself back to taking part in the conversation again, if only listening more attentively.

"I've always wanted to meet a writer. How exciting." Catherine spread the linen napkin across her skirt.

Teddy tucked her napkin inside her collar, letting it drape across her shirt. "Kitty's the middle sister. She maintains the inside of our home. I take care of the farm. Well, it used to just be me, but now Jud helps too." She tapped her fingers on the table.

"Interesting. You'll have to introduce them to me sometime." Catherine took a small sip of water. "I hope to make a good many friends while I'm here. Do you do anything special for Thanksgiving? I can scarcely believe it's only a week away."

What did she mean by 'while I'm here'? Surely, she planned to stay, or had he made that poor an impression on her already?

"Most times, Paul's family and ours get together to

celebrate the holiday." Teddy snuck a glance at him. Something flashed in her eyes that he didn't recognize.

"Does that mean we'll both be joining you this year?" Catherine turned a hopeful gaze toward him.

"What do you say, Teddy?" Paul leaned forward.

"I, uh..." Teddy swallowed a few times and glanced at him.

Odd. He'd never seen her not want to have him come to her place before. After all, there was a well-worn path between their two farms.

He stilled.

A path that wouldn't be traveled very often if he ended up marrying Catherine—at least not by him. Why had he never considered it before?

Chapter Seven

"Y ou did what?"

Teddy cringed at Essie's tone. "We've always invited Paul and his family for Thanksgivin'." She didn't meet her sister's gaze. Had Essie noticed the tick in Teddy's jaw?

Kitty wrapped her arm around Teddy's waist. "I think it's a fine thing you did, asking both Paul and Catherine to join us. I'm sure it wasn't easy seeing the two of them together."

Essie waved her hand as if she were flicking away a swarm of gnats. "Don't mind me. Carrying this baby makes me testy at times."

Kitty and Teddy exchanged a look, and they both struggled to keep from grinning. Essie's emotions flopped all over the place from day to day, and one never knew what she'd come up with during any conversation.

"What? I can't help it." Essie yanked out a chair, collapsing into it. "You'll both understand when you're increasing."

Kitty wrung her hands.

Teddy wanted to kick something.

"I'm sorry. There I go, saying the wrong thing again. Jud and I pray for you both each night, that you'll find godly men like I have."

Was Essie trying to get rid of them so she and Jud could have the house to themselves? Teddy cleared her throat. Maybe it was high time she followed through and started making plans for her future.

"Now don't get the wrong idea. Either of you." Essie studied her younger sisters. "We have no desire to push you away. We're family. It's my prayer we can all settle close to each other when you two get married, and if you never decide to wed, you're always welcome here. It's *our* home." Essie reached her hands out toward Teddy and Kitty.

Kitty swiped away tears and then grasped Essie's hand. "You're forgiven."

Teddy huffed but reached for her sister's other hand.

"You did the right thing by inviting Paul and his fiancée." Essie's face eased into a smile.

Teddy cringed at her sister's choice of word. He hadn't pinned himself to the easterner yet, but it would only be a matter of time. She'd best remember that. It'd been hard enough playing chaperone for a few days. She couldn't imagine what it would be like to see them together all the time.

Essie squeezed her hand. "I don't know that I could've done what you did by asking them for the holiday next week. You don't talk about it, but I'm sure you're heartbroken."

Moisture pricked at the back of her eyes. She ripped her

hand from Essie's grasp and strutted toward the door. "I best see to the livestock." She was out the door before either of her sisters had a chance to respond.

The last thing Teddy wanted was to have a woman's reaction and turn into a puddle of tears. That was something her older sisters would do, but not her. She took pride in keeping a tight rein on her emotions. In fact, she'd been successful at keeping them under the covers until they started this complete nonsense about her caring for Paul. She should never have allowed herself to start thinking like a woman. Clearly no good had come from it.

Teddy glanced at the sky. Clouds mostly covered the low afternoon sun. *I know You're there, Lord, but right now You seem a long way off. I need Your strength to get through this because I can't do it on my own. Other times I've been able to, but now ...*

"I'll leave you two for now, and I'll be back in a couple of hours to take Miss McDougal back to town."

"Thanks, Jud." Paul waved as Essie's husband slapped the reins across the horses' backs. He turned toward Catherine with a smile. "I know the ground looks different now without seeing crops growing, but I hope you can still see the beauty of the land." He stood a little taller. "It's something Pa and I took great pride in."

She sniffed and buried her hands in a fur muff. "It's rather primitive out here, isn't it?"

He glanced around. The afternoon sunlight shimmered

off the water pump, washing the homestead in a gentle tone. "I wouldn't exactly call it primitive. Pa and I worked hard to get this farm up and running."

"Oh, don't get me wrong. It's nice, in a rustic sort of way."

His brow quirked. What exactly did *that* mean? "Well, let me show you the house." He shifted the crutches under his armpits and headed toward it.

Catherine followed beside him, her gaze darting from side to side as she walked.

When he got to the steps, he expected her to stay alongside him like Teddy always did, to make sure he didn't stumble. Instead, she went on up the steps and waited for him by the door, tapping her foot. When he got there, he figured she'd open it for him, but again, she paused and just stared at him until he swung the door open.

Once they were inside, he closed the door behind them. He made a sweeping motion. "Here's the kitchen."

She appeared to look at every single item lining the area. "You don't have fresh water inside?" A stark expression crossed her face.

"No, that's why we have the pump outside, or you can walk to the creek if need be."

She fanned herself with her hand, her face paling.

He moved toward the sitting room, and she followed him without a word.

She strode straight to the cupboard that held Ma's fancy dishes. "These are beautiful. You have exquisite taste. Did you purchase them for me?" Her face beamed.

Paul tugged at his collar. "Uh, no. Those were my mother's. When she moved to Texas to be with my sister and her family, Ma figured she wouldn't need them any longer, so she left them here for me."

"Oh." She deflated like a cake taken from the oven too soon.

"There are three bedrooms as well." He motioned towards them. "Feel free to go and take a peek."

It was a good thing that Teddy had picked up and cleaned the house this week before Catherine arrived. Teddy had said it'd be her last time to help since he'd soon be cast-free and able to take care of things on his own.

Catherine didn't enter any of the bedrooms, but poked her head into each of the doorways before she joined him again. "It's a pleasant home, although rather small."

"Small? I'll have you know my house is one of the biggest in the area." He struggled to rein in the anger that bubbled to the surface.

One of her eyebrows lifted as she studied him.

"Just how *large* was your home?" He realized there were few things he knew about Catherine's background.

"We have two sitting rooms, a formal dining room, a small family dining room, Papa's office, the kitchen, a summer kitchen, and servants' quarters, eight bedrooms, and two...um... bathing rooms." A pink tinge touched Catherine's face as she hurried on. "There also are quite a few outbuildings, a rose garden, riding paths, and, of course, stables."

"With all that, why did you want to come west?"

Her cheeks turned a darker shade of pink. "Papa wanted me to marry a man that I didn't care for, and—"

"Did you run away from home?"

She didn't meet his gaze. "Not exactly. I left a note."

He shoved his fingers through his hair. "Does your pa even know where you were going?"

Her back stiffened, and fire shone in her eyes. "I told him I was coming west. I've read about it so often and wanted to see for myself what it was like."

He hefted a sigh. "This has been a lark for you then. You didn't really plan on marrying me."

She placed her slim fingers on his arm. "There's no reason to get all testy. I wanted to see the West, but also your letter and advertisement in the newspaper intrigued me. It's why I came. You were willing to have a trial period instead of getting married first thing like most men I corresponded with wanted. We still haven't had enough time to really get to know each other."

Paul wasn't so sure that their differences wouldn't be a stumbling block in the future. He should've found out more about her before he sent for her. If things didn't work with Catherine, he doubted he had enough money saved up to ship for another potential bride out here until after the fall harvest next year, and that all depended on whether or not he had a good crop. He scrubbed his hand down his face and wished Jud would return sooner than the two hours he'd mentioned before he had left.

CHAPTER EIGHT

Teddy studied her reflection as Kitty shoved the last pin into the knot of hair at the nape of Teddy's neck. "I still don't see why you want me wearin' a dress today. It's not like I'm goin' to snag Paul's attention when he'll already have a gal on his arm."

"I know that, but I just thought since it's Thanksgiving, we should all dress up this year. From what you mentioned about Catherine, it sounds like she comes from high society."

"Not sure what that is or why it matters." Teddy grumbled under her breath. "Don't think I want to find out either."

"Besides, we don't want her thinking we're a bunch of country bumpkins."

"What's wrong with that?" Teddy patted her hair and stood. "We live in the country, don't we? You wouldn't catch me livin' in the city." She shuddered at the thought.

"We'd better hurry and help Essie with the meal before she wears herself out." Kitty smoothed her skirt as they left the room.

They'd no sooner stepped into the kitchen when a knock sounded. Jud strode across the floor and opened the door. "Hello there, folks. We're so glad you could join us for the day. Happy Thanksgiving, Miss McDougal, Paul." He shook Paul's hand and then helped Catherine with her coat. "How did you two get here? I was just getting ready to hitch the wagon and come fetch you."

Paul hung his coat on a peg by the door. "Catherine hired someone from town to bring her to the farm to pick me up and bring us here. Although I hoped that either you or Teddy could give us a ride home." His gaze swung toward her.

Teddy ignored him and snagged Catherine's hand, tugging her closer to her siblings. "Cattie, I wanted you to meet my sisters."

"It's not Cattie, it's Catherine. I never could abide nicknames." The young woman sniffed and lifted her nose a smidge.

"Sorry about that, *Catherine.*" Teddy glanced at her oldest sister.

Essie stepped forward and held her hand out. "Hello, I'm Essie." She motioned behind her. "And this is Kitty. We're pleased to meet you."

Kitty gave a little curtsy while Essie and Catherine shook hands.

Catherine's face wreathed in a smile. "Everything smells divine. Your cook has outdone herself." She gazed back down the short hallway toward the bedrooms. "I don't see her anywhere. Did she make the meal and leave already?"

Teddy snorted and slapped her knee. "You're lookin' at the cooks."

The city woman's lower lip gaped before she caught it with her teeth. "You mean you make all your own meals? Where do you find the time between your writing and social functions?"

Kitty gestured toward a chair. "There aren't too many social functions around here, although if you're here in February, the town has a sweetheart dance. The church has some picnics when the weather is nice, but otherwise that's about it. I've always longed to have a quilting circle, but most women are too busy taking care of their own households, sewing, and feeding their children to socialize much other than at church."

Catherine gasped. "You can't be serious. Why I've never had a week without my schedule full of different gatherings, dances, or meetings."

"I think you'll find folks live more simply here, Catherine." Paul leaned against the dry sink.

"If you ladies have the grub about ready, I'll set the table." Jud started tugging dishes from the cupboard.

"You don't have maids to take care of all this?" Again, Catherine glanced around their small home.

A laugh tumbled from Teddy's lips. "We do things ourselves. Like I told you before, Kitty helps to slop the pigs, feed the chickens, and takes care of feedin' and clothin' us. Jud and I deal with the larger animals and the farm while Essie does her writin'. We each have a part in helpin'. Besides, there's no room for anybody else since all we have is what you see here and two bedrooms back the hall there."

Catherine's face paled. "That's it? I couldn't abide such primitive living."

Teddy's cheeks burned. "You might find it primitive, but we got each other. Why would we need much more than that?" She turned to help Jud with setting the table, while Essie and Kitty started dishing the food into bowls.

Paul couldn't help comparing Catherine with Teddy as she and her sisters scurried to get the feast on the table. His intended sat like a queen in her chair watching her subjects scamper about finalizing preparations for the feast. He released a breath. Just because the woman had no experience with living on the prairie or taking care of a household didn't mean she couldn't eventually learn how to do those things. Teddy hadn't known how to do a lot of those tasks either until she'd started taking care of him.

His stomach rumbled as turkey and gravy were carried to the table along with a bowl, holding a huge mound of potatoes. He shifted his hip so he didn't bump the pies waiting on the dry sink. Usually Kitty made them, but maybe Teddy had tried her hand at one this year. She'd become mighty handy at domestic tasks, and he already knew she was a hard worker on the farm. There'd been plenty of years where she'd helped to harvest crops and could easily keep up with the menfolk, pulling her weight.

Jud's voice snagged him from his musing. "I think we're about ready. If you'll all take your seats, I'll say the blessing."

"I've never met people who pray other than clergy. I suppose you feel obligated to do so because of the holiday?" Catherine's brow rose as she folded her hands in her lap.

Teddy's face screwed up. "What a funny question. We pray before all our meals and lots of other times too. Prayer's an important part of our lives."

"How quaint. I thought it was only the minister who did such a thing." Catherine reached for the cloth napkin and spread it across the shiny fabric of her dress. The gown was bedecked with all kinds of fancy frippery.

"Let's pray." Jud bowed his head once they all had taken their seats. "Lord, we thank You for Your bountiful gifts. We thank You for family and friends. Thank You for our country. Guide our president. Give him wisdom as he leads our nation. May we always be thankful for the freedom we have in You. In Your Son's name we pray, amen."

Paul lifted his head and found Teddy's gaze on him. Her homespun dress was likely one of her sister's. The blue gingham made her eyes seem larger than normal. She'd put her hair up again, and she looked downright pretty. Some fella would find her irresistible someday. He wished it could be him, but he'd made a commitment to seeing if things would work with Catherine, and he owed it to her to follow through. Pa had taught him to be a man who stuck by his word and fulfill his promises. He'd stick to that, no matter how hard it was.

He broke eye contact with Teddy and busied himself with piling his plate with each food as items were passed. As good as everything had smelled a few minutes ago, he found he barely noticed what it tasted like as he shoveled in forkfuls.

"If you all pray so often, I suppose you attend church regularly as well." Catherine dabbed her mouth with her napkin.

"Yes, don't you?" Essie handed him the basket of rolls.

"Rarely. There's a pew with our family name on it at the church in our city, but Papa and I usually only attended when he was trying to maneuver a business deal with one of the parishioners. The minister tends to drone on for hours and hours." Catherine yawned, patting her lips. "I'm afraid I found it frightfully boring."

"Pastor Wentworth isn't like that." Kitty shot a glance at Teddy. "He always gives sermons you can apply to your life. He and his wife are sweet. We missed you at the service this past Sunday. Hopefully, you'll be able to attend in a few days. We'd love to have you."

"I was simply too exhausted from my travels to come last week. I suppose I can stop in for a visit on Sunday, although I'm not making any promises." Catherine took a small sip of water. "Everything is delicious. Thank you for inviting me. Papa and I would have an elaborate meal if I were home today, but this is still quite good. Although I don't see how you manage without a cook. I simply must have one, as well as a maid, when I marry." She glanced at him.

Paul squirmed in his seat. If he ended up wed to Catherine, he had a feeling he'd constantly be having to buy things to satisfy her. Funny. Ma had never been that way, and she came from the east too. But what concerned him the most was Catherine's lack of a spiritual background and a personal faith in God. It was something he couldn't and wouldn't compromise on. How was he going to tell the woman he didn't think things were going to work between them and still honor the promise he'd made to her?

CHAPTER NINE

W e need to talk." Catherine's gaze flitted to his and then to the twisted hands in her lap.

He glanced around the dining room of the small diner. It was early, and few had ventured outside yet. "What about?" *Perhaps the fact that I can't marry you when you don't share my faith?* He'd been thinking about it for the past couple of days and had yet to find a gentle way to withdraw from their unspoken engagement.

She took a small sip of her coffee and grimaced, shoving it away. "I don't think it's going to work between us."

Relief shot through every pore of his body. "Why do you say that?"

Catherine squirmed in her straight-back chair and followed the pattern on the tablecloth with the tip of her right index finger. "You seem to be a nice man, don't get me wrong, but I'm accustomed to a finer life than this." Her hand fluttered as she motioned toward the window. "I thought I could live a primitive existence like you all do, but I truly don't think I'd be happy here. It isn't fair to you. Besides, I'm sure when I get back home, Papa will understand my concerns with the man he's chosen for me and will allow me to make my own decisions regarding whom I marry. By now he'll be missing me, and he'll listen to what I have to share this time."

"I don't know what to say." He fiddled with the collar of his shirt.

"I'm sure you can see it's for the best. Besides, you can't marry me when you already care for Teddy. Although I don't know what you see in her." She shivered as if she'd taken a sudden chill. "Why you'd want a rough woman like her is beyond me."

"You're mistaken. There's nothing going on between me and Teddy."

Catherine's gaze pinned him. "I'm not blind, Paul Baker. I've seen the way you both look at each other when you think nobody is watching. My guess is, neither of you has realized it, or admitted you care for one another more than as a 'friend.' Honestly." She rolled her eyes.

"We haven't ever talked about such a thing."

She reached over and patted his hand. "Perhaps it's time you did." She smiled and pushed back her chair. "I've enjoyed getting to know you, Paul, and learning more about the West. It's made me realize how much I treasure my life back home. Thank you for sending for me, even though it didn't work out the way we thought. I'll be sure Papa reimburses you for the cost of my train fare once I arrive home. Goodbye, Paul." She leaned down and kissed him on the cheek. "Best wishes."

He sat there for a few minutes after she left, going over their conversation in his head again. *Thank You, Lord, for providing a way out for me. I would've broken things off if she hadn't, but she certainly made things easier.* The clink of dishes in the kitchen stirred his attention back to where he sat. *You know I've tried to put away the feelings I have for Teddy and follow what Ma wanted for me, but I guess I never stopped and asked You about it. What're Your plans for me when it comes to picking a wife? Will You please show me?*

Paul stood and slipped the crutches under his armpits. He flicked a few coins onto the table.

Moments later, he breathed in deeply of the frigid December air as he stepped onto the wooden walkway. His crutches thudded with each step as he headed toward Doc's place. Just as he reached the office, he saw Teddy swing down from her horse over near the livery. She glanced his way but didn't come over to him. Instead, she turned away.

Odd. She'd never ignored him before.

He shrugged and pushed open the door. His neighbor, who lived on the other side of Paul, had brought him to town early this morning and would head back home in another hour. Hopefully, it wouldn't take long at the doctor.

"Good to have you here, Paul." Mrs. Master, the doc's ma, smiled at him. She sat at a small desk in the waiting room. Chairs lined the walls on two sides. For now, they were empty. "My son was figuring he'd have to ride out to your place today to see about getting the cast off. We didn't expect you to be visiting town while still encumbered with crutches."

Paul removed his hat and hung it on a peg. "One of my

neighbors brought me along with him this morning."

"I imagine so you could visit your sweetheart, although I can't see how you've chosen a fancy woman over Teddy Love. You both are like two fingers in a glove. You belong together."

"Mother. It's none of our business." Doc's short, stocky body leaned against the doorway leading into his office.

The woman tsked but said nothing further.

"Come on in. Good to see you, Paul. How's that leg doing?"

"Hasn't hurt a bit." Paul followed the doc and hopped onto the examination table.

"Hope you brought an extra pair of pants. Otherwise, your pant leg will flop everywhere." Doc stared at him over his spectacles and reached for a saw.

"Got it in my bag here." He plopped a burlap sack beside him. "I sure won't miss this thing." He thunked the cast one last time.

Minutes later, Paul felt about ten pounds lighter as he slid off the table and stood on both feet. He couldn't stop a grin from spreading.

Doc pushed and prodded on his limb. "Does this hurt at all?"

"Nope. Feels just fine. Although the muscle's a bit weak."

"That's to be expected. Take your time getting back to normal activity around the farm. When your leg hurts," he glanced at Paul over his glasses again, "and it will ache, make sure you put it up and rest. Got it?"

"You've got it, Doc. I'm just happy to be back on my own two feet again." He took a few tentative steps.

A chuckle rumbled from Doc. "Guess you're champing at the bit to marry your mail-order bride."

Paul shook his head. "No, I'm afraid it didn't work out between us."

Doc clapped him on the shoulder and then started cleaning up. "Sorry to hear that."

"I'm not. Turns out we had differences that couldn't be settled between us. In fact, she broke things off with me right before I came here."

The balding man stopped what he was doing and stared at Paul. "You don't seem heartbroken by it."

He shook his head. "No. I'm thankful the Lord intervened. We wouldn't have been happy together."

"I'd like to say it's a shame, but maybe it's God's way of clearing the path for you to marry Teddy instead."

Paul's head came up. "You think she'd have me after I've been chasing after another woman?"

"I don't have experience in that area, but I imagine if you sweet-talk her, she'll come around."

He scrubbed a hand across his forehead. "I don't know, Doc. Teddy isn't like most gals. I'm not sure sweet-talking will make a difference with her."

"Well, you'll have to find some way to snag her attention."

The question was, what would speak to Teddy and turn her heart toward him?

"What do you mean you're moving?" Confusion lined

Teddy's brother-in-law's face. "I hope I haven't made you feel you're no longer wanted or needed here." Jud rubbed the back of his neck.

Teddy turned to him.

"What's going on?" Kitty crossed the room and snaked her arm around Teddy's waist.

"You can't leave." Essie's eyes filled with tears. "We all have to stay together."

Jud placed an arm around his wife's shoulders. "Now, Angel, your sisters have the right to do as they please. They're both adults."

Essie sniffed, tugging a handkerchief from her skirt pocket. "When are you planning to leave?"

Teddy glanced at her family. Leaving them would be the hardest thing she'd ever done. "Right after Christmas. I'd leave sooner, but I know how important the holiday is to you and Kitty and figured you wouldn't want me departin' before then."

Kitty hugged her and then grasped her hand, studying Teddy's eyes. "You're leaving because of Paul and Catherine, aren't you?"

She winced and then nodded. "I can't stay here and see them day in and day out. There was an older couple in town today. They live about twenty miles from here. I heard them askin' around to see if anyone would be interested in helpin' them with their farm. They don't have any children." She glanced at each of her loved ones. "If things work out, they may at some point hand the farm over to me. It's not a guarantee, but at least I'd be earnin' money I can set aside for purchasin' my own place, if they don't feel I'm a fit for them. I plan to head out the day after Christmas."

"That means we only have a little over three weeks together." Essie's hand flew to her chest, and she started blinking like crazy again. "You won't be here when the baby arrives."

Jud patted his wife's hand, drawing her close to his side.

Teddy swallowed and looked away from their embrace. As much as she desired to see the little one, it would only be a reminder of what Teddy would never have.

Kitty's face shone with tears, but still a small smile broke through, like the sun breaking through the clouds after a rainstorm. "We want what's best for you, Teddy."

She nodded, not trusting her voice enough to speak.

If only God had agreed on what she had hoped was best for her—Paul Baker. But apparently, it wasn't meant to be.

Chapter Ten

I don't know if I can go over there one last time." Teddy paced in her small bedroom. "Why did Paul send word for me to help him for a couple of days? We saw him almost a week ago at church. He's out of the cast now. Besides, Jud can assist Paul just as well as I can. It don't make no sense if you ask me."

Kitty finished buttoning her shoes and stood. "You're going to go, aren't you? Maybe he has something important to say."

"Not sure I want to hear it. I've already told him I won't make a cake for his weddin'."

Kitty gasped, her lower lip dropping before she snapped it shut. "When did that come up?"

"When I took over the one I made for him before Catherine arrived." She slammed her Stetson in place. "Guess I'd better get it over with."

"Aren't you going to eat breakfast first?" Kitty opened the door.

"No, don't think I could stomach food even if I wanted to. If I'm not back in an hour, maybe you'd better send Jud after me."

Kitty halted her with a hand on her arm. "I'll be praying, Teddy. Trust God to work."

Teddy tried to pray on the short ride to Paul's place, but she could barely string two words together. Hopefully, the Lord could make sense of her thoughts.

She studied the gray sky as she rode. If she hazarded a guess, they'd have snow again before day's end. The clouds billowed one on top of the other, and the air smelled like precipitation was coming. The temperatures were cold enough for it to snow. Her breath puffed out in a small cloud before disappearing.

She reached Paul's farm, the leather of her saddle creaking as she swung down from her horse and tied it to the hitching post. Teddy had her back turned toward the house, but the skritch of the door opening and soft footsteps told her Paul had stepped outside. She squared her shoulders and swiveled to meet his gaze.

"I was afraid you wouldn't come." He held onto the banister as he descended the steps and slowly walked toward her.

"Wasn't sure I would either." She tugged her hat lower over her brow. Clearing her throat, she swallowed past the lump in her throat. "What did you need that Jud couldn't do for you?"

He didn't answer right away, and silence stretched between them.

She glanced at his face.

"I need *you*, Teddy Love."

She stilled, waiting for him to say more.

"I've been doing a lot of thinking and praying the past week or so, particularly since I got my cast off." He took a step closer to her.

"Oh? What about?"

"About what *I* want in a wife, not what *Ma* desires for me."

"I thought you had it all planned when you sent for Catherine."

He shook his head. "No, I was following what Ma had requested before she left Kansas. Should've seen it long before I came up with the mail-order bride idea." He kicked in the dirt with the toe of the boot of his mended leg. "In fact, I did see it, but I didn't think I'd stand a chance with you. Didn't think you'd ever feel that way about me."

He reached over and snagged her hand. She ripped it free from his grasp. "You can't be holdin' my hand when you're plannin' to marry that city gal."

"That's just it, I'm not."

Her gaze darted to his.

A grin spread across his handsome face.

"You're talkin' foolish. Are you sure Doc didn't give you medicine that's makin' you not think straight?"

He laughed and edged closer to her again. "I'm not taking any medicine. Catherine decided we aren't a good fit and headed back from where she came."

"Sorry to hear that."

"You are?" He stole her Stetson from her head and bumped under her chin so she'd look at him.

"N-not really. Just seemed like the thing to say." Teddy

exhaled a blustery breath. She could hardly think straight when his face was mere inches away from hers.

"If she hadn't said something, I would've. You see, Catherine doesn't have the qualities I need in a wife." His eyes twinkled.

She felt a funny hitch in her chest. "W-what things are you needin' in a wife? She was genteel and refined like your ma would've liked."

He reached out and tucked a stray piece of hair behind her ear.

Her stomach flopped as if she were riding a bucking bronco.

"A woman who puts the needs of others before her own, one who isn't afraid to get her hands filthy, to work hard by my side through the good and the bad times. One who makes me laugh and is with me no matter what we face." He paused, his eyes taking on a glow she'd never seen before.

She stared intently at his face, wanting to hear what he had to say next but also afraid.

"Most importantly, I need a woman who's my best friend. I asked you to help me pick a bride. *I pick you, Teddy.*"

Her chest constricted. "But your ma won't be happy when she learns you want me."

He seemed to chew on the thought for a minute. "No. I don't think she'll mind. Her last words to me were to find someone who'd make me happy. Someone I can love with all my heart. I need *you*, Teddy Love, provided you'll have me. Will you marry me?"

She snaked one arm around his waist and tugged him toward her. Her pulse stampeded as she stood on tiptoe and with her other arm pulled his head down and claimed his lips.

Paul's heart bucked as he wrapped his arms around Teddy and shifted her closer, deepening their kiss. His lips moved to her cheek and neck. *Dear Lord, I love her so.*

She tugged back a smidge and brought her hand to his face. "I love you, Paul Baker. Don't rightly know when it started and maybe wouldn't have figured it out if it weren't for my sisters sayin' somethin'."

He threw back his head and laughed. "I've known it for five years but didn't think you'd ever think of me the way a woman loves a man."

"You're jokin'."

"No." His shoulders shook with his laughter. "Ma recognized it too and tried to persuade me to find someone more like her." He reached for her face and cupped it in his palms. "But I don't want a woman like my ma. I want you, Teddy. I love you. Please say yes."

He covered her lips again.

She was breathless when he slowly shifted back an inch or two. "I thought I already did. There's one problem though."

His hand faltered. "What problem could there be?"

"I already told some old folks who live about twenty miles from here that I'd move there and help them with their farm. They plan to pass it on to me if they're happy with my work." Deep lines crossed her face. "They're leaving this mornin' to head back to their place. They've been stayin' in town the past week."

His pulse stuttered. "I'm sure they'll understand when we explain."

"You'll go with me?"

"Of course. I don't plan to let you out of my sight until you tell me when you'll marry me."

She squeezed his hand. "That'll have to wait. I need to head to town now, so I can catch them in time."

"Then let's go. I'll ride behind your saddle."

Teddy barely noticed the scenery as they rode to town and caught up with the old couple. She'd been keenly aware of Paul as his arms encircled her waist. Breathing had been difficult at best with him so close.

She caught sight of the couple as they were heading toward their home and reined her horse beside their wagon.

"Hello there, Teddy. We weren't expecting to see you before we left." The old man pulled the horses to a halt.

The old farmer's wife's eyes shimmered. "Hiram, it looks like we'll need to keep on searching for someone to help with our place."

"What do you mean? I thought Teddy was going to." The old fella stared at her and then at Paul. A grin revealed a couple of missing teeth. "I get it. You decided to stay here and marry. Can't blame you, young'uns."

His wife patted his arm. "Isn't young love something to behold? We wish you two the best." The older couple waved farewell and then started on their way.

Teddy turned her horse toward home, realizing she hadn't even needed to say a single word to them. She couldn't help laughing.

"What is it, Teddy?" Paul's voice rumbled behind her. He reached around her and tugged on the reins. He jumped off the horse and then lifted a hand to assist her as she dropped beside him on the ground.

"I didn't count on it going so well that I didn't even need to speak." She glanced toward the couple as they made their way across the prairie.

"I guess God's working things out for us. Now, about my question. When are you going to marry me?" Paul tugged on her hand.

"How soon do you want to get hitched?" Teddy felt like dancing a little jig.

"The sooner the better, although I suppose your sisters will say they need time to make you a dress."

"There's no need of that."

Paul placed a finger on her lips. "I'd like to see you in a wedding dress, with your hair all fancy like when you brought me the cake."

"You said you liked it down, not up." She planted her hands on her hips. "Were you lyin' to me, Paul Baker?"

His cheeks flushed. "You might say that. At the time, I couldn't let you know how much it affected me seeing you dressed like that."

Her heart did a happy little jolt. "Are you keepin' any

other secrets from me?"

His head wagged from side to side. "Let's get married two days before Christmas. That way, we can celebrate our first holiday together. Two weeks should give your sisters plenty of time to make you something fancy." He leaned in for a kiss.

Teddy's heart pattered as she turned her cheek toward him, afraid the whole thing was a dream. Had Paul said what she'd thought, or had she imagined his interest? The last thing she needed was to turn all sappy like her sisters.

"I know you've always wanted a place of your own, Teddy." He brushed his lips across her forehead. "I hope you find that with me."

Her pulse thudded as she studied his face.

Teddy couldn't deny the devotion and passion shining in Paul's brown eyes.

She drew his head down again, not waiting for his lips to claim hers, instead tugging him closer and sealing her love on his mouth and cheeks. Her heart swelled with love for this man. She had surely found a home of her own with Paul.

EPILOGUE

December 23, 1876

Teddy ran her fingers along the side of her skirt a second time. "Are you sure this isn't too much? Paul won't recognize me in this getup."

Kitty laughed and tugged Teddy in a quick hug before stepping back. "He'll think you look beautiful."

Teddy stared at her reflection one more time. Kitty had twisted, curled, and done Teddy didn't know what to her hair, but little curls framed the side of her face and a bunch piled high on her head with a few springing out and boinging down the back of the blue satin dress.

Essie poked her head inside the door. "Are you two about finished? We need to get seated, Kitty, so Jud can walk her down the aisle. By the way, you look gorgeous, Teddy. Paul won't be able to keep his eyes off you." She gave a little wave and left.

"I'm coming." Kitty gave her a peck on the cheek and whispered, "I'm so happy for you, Teddy. I pray that when the time is right, you help me see the man God has for me."

"You can count on it." Teddy winked at her sister.

Jud knocked on the door and then stepped inside. "Are you ready?"

She nodded as Kitty slipped from the small room.

"He's a good man, Teddy." Jud jutted his elbow for her to take. "I'm glad things worked out for you two."

"Me too." Her heart hammered in her chest as they stood at the back of the church.

Bright red ribbons and bows hung at the end of each pew. A Christmas tree graced the corner of the room, but what she couldn't keep her eyes off was her best friend standing at the end of the aisle.

She trotted up the aisle, tugging Jud along behind her.

Paul grinned from ear to ear as he waited at the altar for his choice of a bride.

Teddy couldn't be happier. Her best friend had finally come to his senses.

COURTING LOVE

WOOING THE COOK

But if ye forgive not men their trespasses, neither will your Father forgive your trespasses.

Matthew 6:15 (KJV)

CHAPTER ONE

January 22, 1877,
Yoder Grove, Kansas

T he fellas are giving you until the end of the day to find a new cook, or they're leaving."

Noah Eldridge scrubbed the back of his neck with his hand trying to ease the knots his foreman's words had stirred. "I take it things aren't working out with Shorty?"

"You and I both know he belongs in the saddle and not in the kitchen." Henry Kierman, the man who'd been helping with the cattle ranch ever since Noah could remember, frowned at him. Henry had been a blessing ever since Pa's passing six months ago. "Don't know why you thought the old cowpoke would be a good fit."

"He needed a break from the saddle after the horse threw him last month and cracked his ribs." Noah had thought the man would've been able to come up with at least one decent meal, but so far it hadn't happened. "Don't suppose you've heard of any cookies in the area who need a job?"

"I'd be the first one lined up to talk to him if there were one." Henry stared at the horizon as if hoping one would appear.

"Is the cook from the diner in town still around?"

Henry shook his head. "Heard tell he left a few days after it closed."

"I don't know who else to ask." Noah ran a hand along his short beard.

"You and I both know the one lady who could fill the position."

Noah refrained from squirming under his foreman's steady gaze. "She isn't an option." *Unfortunately.*

"The fellas are always the first in line to eat her baked goods at the annual sweetheart dance. Folks know she has a reputation for making delicious chow. I'm not sure what happened between you two when you were young, but it's high time to set that aside and ask Miss Love to help." The silver streaks in Henry's dark hair glittered in the sun as he removed his Stetson, banging it against his thigh, dust billowing from the hat.

Just the mention of Kitty Love's cooking made Noah's gut churn. He heaved a breath, causing a mist to circle his head in the brisk morning air. If he didn't know better, they'd have snow before the day ended.

Shorty led King from the barn, handing the reins to Noah. "Here, boss. Henry said you'll be heading to town for supplies and to talk to Miss Love afterwards." His dark brows waggled. "Make sure you sweet-talk her so we can finally have something good to eat."

Noah glared at his foreman.

At least the man had the decency to look chagrined.

He bit back a groan as he swung onto the saddle. "Don't let the men leave. I'll come up with someone to cook the victuals tonight." Even if he had to do it himself. How hard could it be to fry up a slab of bacon and cook a big pot of beans?

The saddle creaked as Noah turned his mount toward Yoder Grove.

King tossed his head, jingling the buckles on the bridle.

"Sorry, boy." He loosened his tight grip on the reins. "Guess my thoughts were elsewhere."

King snorted.

"How am I going to get Kitty to agree to come to the ranch?"

His stallion didn't give a response.

"She's never forgiven me for how I teased her incessantly in the schoolroom." He hadn't been able to help himself. She squeaked when he hid a mouse in her desk in their second year of school. Screamed when he dipped her blonde braids into his inkwell the third year. Stomped on his foot in fourth grade after he tied her and her apron strings to the flagpole when they had been playing hide and seek during recess. The following year, they had a new teacher, and Noah had been seated on the opposite side of the schoolroom. Mr. Wilder was a hard taskmaster, often rapping the knuckles of his students with a ruler with very little reasoning behind it. Noah hadn't wanted to risk getting in trouble, so he'd behaved that year.

In their sixth year at the one-room school, Miss Mueller replaced Mr. Wilder, and Noah had returned to his

163

shenanigans with Kitty. He put a frog in her lunch pail. She cried when it jumped onto her lap. The pranks blurred after that. Noah tried to do whatever he could to get a rise out of Kitty before they both graduated in eighth grade. He recognized then and now that he'd only played the tricks on her not because of her reactions, but because Noah liked her.

He groaned. "What little boy knows how to treat a girl when he cares about her? They do the same things to a gal they do for the fellas they're friends with." Maybe Kitty never understood that since she only had sisters, and as far as he could tell, she only preferred the company of other women. Either way, it didn't matter. She hadn't spoken to him since they'd left school, except if she was forced to be civil at church. Even then, she merely said, "Good day." Never meeting his gaze.

"Lord, You know I've tried to apologize to her many times through the years since then, but she never stays in my presence more than a few seconds. How am I ever going to get her to forgive me, let alone agree to come to the ranch and cook for the hands?"

Kitty Love closed the door behind her so she wouldn't wake her new niece. As much as she loved living with her oldest sister, Essie, and her husband, Jud, Kitty couldn't help feeling like she was in the way since the baby had arrived. Their two-bedroom farmhouse suddenly seemed too small. Granted, it would be a while before the baby would need space of her own. Still.

There must be something I can do to earn a living, Lord. At least until You see fit to bring a man into my life. You know I've always wanted to be married like Essie and Teddy. It had been almost a month since her baby sister had married their next-door neighbor, Paul Baker.

And here I thought I'd be the first one to get married.

She shoved open the barn door.

Jud came from a stall. "Did Essie or Miriam need me?" His brow puckered.

"They both are fine. Just thought I'd head into town for some supplies."

"Would you like me to harness the wagon for you?"

"I can do it." She set her basket aside on a stack of hay.

"It's no problem."

Moments later, Jud led the team from the barn. He lifted her onto the high bench seat. "Don't be too long. I have a feeling it might snow later."

She gave a nod and released the brake. "I'm sure I'll be home well before suppertime. There's a stew on the stove, and the bread is rising." She clicked, and the horse and wagon set in motion.

Kitty mentally went over her list as the short mile quickly passed beneath the wheels. The sound of dry prairie grass crunching filled the morning air.

Ten minutes later, she brought the conveyance to a halt in front of the dry goods store. With a sigh, Kitty glanced around the small town. *If only the diner hadn't closed at the beginning of the year, Lord. Otherwise, they might have needed an additional cook. I guess our town isn't big enough to support a business like that.*

Securing the reins at the hitch post, Kitty hurried into the store.

"Howdy, Miss Love. How can I help you today?" Thomas Warren limped toward her.

"What happened, Mr. Warren?" She set her basket on the counter and touched the older man's arm. "It seems like you're the one who could use some assistance. I could work for you, that is if you need someone." Kitty took a deep breath.

The gray-haired man chuckled. "I just slept wrong." He stretched his back. "The kinks will be gone before long. I'm getting too old for this. Good thing my grandson will be arriving from Kansas City in a week or two on the stagecoach."

Kitty's pulse quickened. What were the chances of Mr. Warren's grandson being interested in staying in the town and maybe finding a bride? She cleared her throat. "Will he be bringing his family too?"

The morning light glimmered off the shopkeeper's bald head as he wagged it from side to side. "Just him. I keep telling him he needs to marry, but the boy says he's not interested. Maybe once he tastes some of your cooking, he'll change his mind." He waggled his gray eyebrows.

Heat crept up Kitty's neck, flooding her cheeks and making her feel as if the store's woodstove had been stoked a good twenty degrees or more since her arrival. She bent her head, tugging the list from her coat pocket.

Mr. Warren chuckled. "Are you trying to find a job?

Hadn't realized your family was struggling financially."

Her lips pinched together. The last thing she needed was for the man to be spreading rumors about them. "No, sir. I just figured to make my own way now since both Essie and Teddy are married."

His lips twitched. "Never figured of the three of you, you'd be the last one to get hitched."

Neither did I, but the Good Lord hasn't seen fit to bring anyone into my life just yet. Not that she could share *that* information with the store owner though. She reread her list again.

"Did you want me to gather items for you while you do other shopping in town?"

The breath she hadn't known she'd been holding, released in a gush. "No, thank you. Why don't you rest, and I'll gather what I need." *Thank You, Lord, that he didn't mention anything else about me being a spinster.*

"How's the new baby doing?" Mr. Warren settled on a wooden stool. "Doc told me about it, but he didn't mention the name Essie and Jud picked."

Kitty hefted a sack of sugar and a small tin of baking powder and set them on the counter. "They called her Miriam."

"Guess it will be a bit before they bring her to town, especially with it being in the middle of winter." He folded his arms across his wide belly. "Always wished my Emelia and I could've had more children than our son. At least he's made up for it and has had a passel of young'uns."

Kitty selected a bottle of molasses and added it to her pile. "How many grandchildren do you have now, Mr. Warren?"

"Ten." The shopkeeper's chest puffed. "Winston's the

oldest. He's the one who'll be coming soon."

The bell above the door to the store jingled merrily.

Kitty turned toward the front with a smile tugging her cheeks until she glimpsed *him*. With a huff, she presented her back to Noah Eldridge and stared unseeingly at the list gripped tight in her hand. *Why did he have to show up, Lord?*

The screech of Mr. Warren's stool scraping across the floor sounded. "Hello, Noah."

She didn't particularly need anything in the back of the store, but now seemed like a good time to see if the shopkeeper had new items on the shelves. Anything to get away from the troublemaker who had teased her all throughout their school years. Moisture pricked at the corner of Kitty's eyes as she hurried away from the two men. She flicked away a tear.

Pull yourself together. There's no reason to get all teary over something that happened years ago. More than likely, Noah has completely forgotten how horrible he was in the past. Finish your shopping and get on your way without talking to him, and you'll be fine.

She peeked around a display of assorted farm equipment.

His hazel-eyed gaze caught hers for a second before she ducked down.

Her heart hammered a staccato beat, echoing the thrumming in her temples.

Maybe he hasn't seen me.

Boots tapped a steady clatter against the wooden floor as someone grew closer.

Lord, is it too much to ask You to prevent him from seeing me?

She crouched lower, squeezing her eyes shut. *Don't let him see me. Please don't let him see me.*

"Did you drop something on the floor?"

His deep voice yanked Kitty from her delusion that Noah hadn't observed her other than his initial glance.

She wobbled, losing her balance and grabbing for the nearest thing to keep from falling to the floor and making the situation any worse than it already was.

Kitty gripped a set of shears, crying out as the sharp blade sliced into her palm. The pile of tools shook before crashing to the floor around her.

He tugged her to her feet, away from the tumbling equipment.

Tears welled in her eyes, splashing down her cheeks. Kitty bit back a sob. "Look what you did."

CHAPTER TWO

Noah's gut tightened as he fished a handkerchief from
his pocket, thankful he'd placed a fresh one there this
morning before leaving the house. "Here, let me help you."
He reached for Kitty's hand, wrapping the cloth around the
cut on it. The wound didn't appear to be too deep, but he
still put a little pressure on it to staunch the bleeding.

"Ouch. You're hurting me." Moisture welled in Kitty's
deep blue eyes as she tried to tug her hand free.

He held fast. "I'm just trying to help you."

"It'd be the first time," she muttered under her breath.

Noah chose to ignore her barb since her words held more
truth than not.

"What happened here?" Thomas Warren shuffled toward
them. He wagged his head from side to side. "Going to take
me a while to set things right."

"I'm sorry, Mr. Warren. I will pick it all up." Kitty's lower
lip trembled.

"No need to fret about that just yet." Noah peeked under

the handkerchief. The blood flow already seemed to slow. Just for good measure, he continued to put pressure on the wound.

This time Kitty winced but didn't tug or pull away. Maybe she'd be a bit more open to his job suggestion than he'd hoped. The question was how to bring it up without ruffling her feathers any.

"How're things going at the ranch, Noah? One of your men mentioned they were thinking of leaving." Thomas leaned against the edge of a case filled with canned goods.

"They aren't happy with our current cook." Noah considered how much he should mention.

"Well, isn't that a fine coincidence?" The shopkeeper grinned, his eyes twinkling. "Miss Love was just asking me for a job. I bet your men would enjoy her being your full-time cook."

Noah's gaze darted to meet hers.

Her face paled.

Did it have anything to do with the cut, or the thought of spending more time in his presence? Noah wasn't sure he wanted to know the answer to his question. "They, uh, aren't happy with Shorty. In fact, I came to town to see if I could find someone who'd be willing to cook for a bit." He didn't dare meet Kitty's eyes this time.

"Considering Miss Love is such an incredible cook, your men will eat fine fare every day." Mr. Warren leaned closer. "If you ask me, it's an answer to prayer for both of you." He motioned his pudgy finger toward Kitty. "Miss Love needs a job, and you're looking to hire a cook."

Guess I don't need to come outright and ask after all, Lord.

Although it couldn't hurt to do a little convincing. "I promise it won't be for long, Kitty... just until I can advertise in the newspaper and someone accepts. You wouldn't be helping me as much as you'd be helping the fellas." Noah chanced a look at her.

She sucked in a noisy breath. "I don't know..."

Noah's pulse thudded in his temples. She was going to refuse unless he came up with something quickly to persuade her. But what?

"Sounds like it's the neighborly thing to do if you ask me." Mr. Warren shifted on his feet. "I remember your ma, Miss Love. She was always faithful in helping others. You remind me of her."

That might be one way of swaying Kitty, reminding her of her ma. Too bad Noah hadn't thought of it. Of course, the words were likely to be better accepted by the storekeeper than if they had come from Noah.

"Well..." She nibbled on her bottom lip, her gaze darting to Mr. Warren. "I'd hate not to do my Christian duty..." Kitty shot a quick glance at Noah. "You promise you'll advertise for someone right away? That this won't be long term?"

"Absolutely. In fact, I'll stop by the newspaper office before I leave town."

Kitty didn't respond right away, instead staring back and forth between him and Mr. Warren. "I suppose I could assist you for a short time."

She swallowed so loudly Noah could hear it. He held his breath, afraid that if he said something she'd spook and run out of the store, taking with her his only chance of keeping the men from walking off the job.

"Looks like you two finally mended some fences. Figured it was about time you two came together instead of always being at odds with each other. If you ask me, Miss Love working at the ranch should be a permanent thing. Solves both of your problems. Who knows, maybe the two of you will find out you like each other too." Mr. Warren chuckled and headed toward the front of the store. He turned on his heel, glancing over his shoulder. "I'll be on my stool if you need me. You might want to finish finding the items on your list, Miss Love, so you can start at the ranch right away."

"I'd appreciate it if you could..." Noah removed his Stetson and scrubbed his hand through his hair before replacing the hat. "The fellas have been might hungry." His stomach rumbled.

A small smile tugged at Kitty's cheeks. "I hate to see people not have good food to eat."

His chest eased. He didn't know how it'd happened, but somehow, the storekeeper had convinced her to come to his aid. *Thank You, Lord. I should never have doubted You to work in the situation.*

"I'll need to stop by the farm and tell them where I'll be so they don't worry." She tugged her hand free and started picking up items from the floor, placing them on the small table.

He stooped to assist her. "Whatever you need. How, uh, how's the hand doing?" Noah closed the shears, placing the blade portion toward the back of the display.

"It'll be fine. I'll wash it out when I get home." She set the last tool on the overflowing table. "And you promise to stop by the newspaper office, right?"

He nodded.

"I suppose I'll see you at the ranch then." She turned her back and scurried to the front.

Noah heaved a sigh. Now if only he could convince Kitty to stay on permanently as his ranch cook.

"You did what?"

Kitty bit back a groan. Of all the times for all of her family to be assembled. She'd hoped to slip into the house during Essie and Miriam's nap time and just leave a note explaining the situation. Instead, she'd arrived home to find Teddy and Paul had decided to drop by as well.

"Are you plannin' on answerin' my question?" Teddy wagged her finger back and forth under Kitty's nose, nearly bopping her with it. "Thought you couldn't stand the man."

Essie came alongside Kitty, draping an arm around her. "I remember all the years of your crying on account of the antics of Noah Eldridge. What on earth did he do or say to make you want to go to his ranch and cook for him?"

"I'm not cooking for him." Well, not exactly. "He just needs a cook for a short time until he can find one. It's something Mama would've done." She'd best hang on to that reminder when things got rough. Knowing Noah, he'd find some way to try her patience. Probably on multiple occasions.

"Were you lookin' for a job?" Teddy folded her arms across her chest. "Don't make no sense why you'd volunteer like this."

Paul and Jud watched from their chairs by the kitchen table, not saying anything. The small cradle swayed beside them, which meant even the baby was awake for this conversation.

"I may have mentioned something to Mr. Warren."

"Don't you like helping here?" A tear trickled down Essie's cheeks. "You don't want to be with us?"

Kitty weighed her next words. Her oldest sister had been exceptionally emotional since she'd given birth to Miriam almost two weeks ago. Actually, all the past nine months or so now that Kitty thought about it. She tugged Essie into a hug. "Of course not, silly. I love being with you all... but I'll need to eventually find a way for myself too..." She glanced at both of her sisters. "You each have your own lives now, and I'm happy for you. I'm not planning on staying on as a full-time cook at Noah's ranch, only helping for a short time. You know me, I won't be staying there any longer than need be, but I want to honor Mama's memory by assisting folks like she would've."

Teddy grunted. "I reckon I can respect that."

"I had hoped you'd help with the baby and meals..." Essie sniffed.

Jud stood, crossing the room, wrapping an arm around his wife's waist. "Now, darling, you know I'm here to aid in anything you need." He kissed her forehead before giving Kitty a wink. "Besides, it's a slow time with the farm right now, so you'll probably soon grow tired of having me underfoot while you're writing or caring for the baby's physical needs." Color tinged his cheeks.

Essie stood on tiptoe and planted a kiss on her husband's lips. "You know I'll never grow tired of having you near me."

"I still don't like it." Teddy shook her head.

Paul must've got a hint from Jud because he also crossed the room, wrapping his wife in a hug. "Simmer down, dear. It's a good thing Kitty is trying to forgive things between her and Noah."

I don't know where Paul got that idea. I said nothing about forgiving Noah. This is about honoring Mama's memory and nothing more. But if it meant her sisters would stop fussing at Kitty, she'd accept it.

Her youngest sister visibly relaxed in her husband's arms. Kitty had never seen such a change in Teddy in such a short time.

She couldn't help wondering what it would be like to have a good man standing beside her, guiding her to see the truth, even if it wasn't her first inclination in a stressful situation. *Oh, Lord, You know I long for a relationship like my sisters have. Is it too much to ask You to bring someone like that into my life? Perhaps even at Noah's ranch? Maybe he's hired a new hand who might be interested in me. Surely there's someone You have who would make a suitable mate. I feel like I've been waiting a long time. Not that I'm complaining.* Well, maybe she was. She released a tight breath.

Jud shifted his attention to Kitty. "You'll back out if things aren't going well? You know you're always welcome here, right? It's your home too."

She swiped a tear from her cheek. "I know that... but I realize it won't be long before you need more room here."

Essie placed a hand on her now-flat stomach. "I don't

know that I'm in a hurry for another little one yet, so you have nothing to worry about."

Maybe not, but Kitty still wanted to find a way to support herself and make her own way in the world. She couldn't write novels like Essie, or farm like Teddy, but surely the Good Lord had given Kitty abilities someone would find useful. *Please, Lord. Even if it means I'll be cooking the rest of my life for other people instead of my own family. Please don't make me be an old bitter spinster. Or a young one either.*

Noah glanced at the cuckoo clock on the wall in the bunkhouse. He thought that by now Kitty would've arrived. He couldn't help wondering if she'd changed her mind... or if her sisters had tried to make Kitty go back on her word. *Lord, don't let it be the case. Please allow her to come so I can let her know I've cared about her ever since we were in school.* His Adam's apple bobbed in his throat as he thought more on the matter. *Could You help me persuade her I'm someone she can depend on? To forgive me for all the foolish pranks I played on her as a child?*

He tugged the big pot of beans onto what he hoped was the hottest portion of the cookstove. Now if only he could start the noonday meal without scorching anything. It would be a first. Hopefully, his meal would be enough to tide the men over until Kitty showed up. Noah glanced out the window again.

If she made an appearance.

Chapter Three

K itty's stomach clenched the closer she got to Noah's ranch. What had she done? Her heart galloped unlike her plodding horse. She'd slowed the mare to a walk about a mile ago trying to get up some gumption to follow through with her commitment. Instead, the enormity of her decision tempted her to backtrack the entire way.

Her hands sweated in the soft leather gloves despite the cold temperatures. The mare tossed her head. Kitty forced herself to relax, patting the horse's neck. "Sorry, girl. I didn't mean to take my nerves out on you."

Like it or not, she'd arrived at the LazE Spur Ranch. Kitty passed under the sign.

A cowboy saw her and released a whoop. "She's here!" The man waved his Stetson and rode toward several other fellas a couple hundred yards away.

Kitty hadn't planned on a welcoming committee, least of all from the cowboys. She studied each man as they rode toward her, but none of them was Noah. Breathing a little easier, she swung down from her horse, smoothing her skirts once her feet touched the ground.

"Howdy, Miss Love." Noah's foreman, Henry Kierman, took the reins from her. "Allow me to take care of her for you."

"Thank you." She licked her lips as she glanced around.

"If you're looking for Noah, he's in the bunkhouse. Feel free to go on in. Noah gave the men strict instructions not to go inside whenever you're here." He dipped his Stetson, turning toward the barn. Her mare trailed after him.

"Howdy, Miss." A sandy-haired man swung his hat from his head as he dipped in a bow. "We're so happy you're here."

A dark-haired man with a bushy mustache grinned at her from atop his horse. "Can't wait to taste your chow, Miss."

Another cowboy tipped his Stetson. Four more were heading across the pasture. Dozens of longhorn cattle ignored them as the men passed by, waving their hats in greeting.

Just how many men did Noah employ?

Kitty swallowed. In all her life, she'd never been welcomed in such a way. *I think I'll enjoy cooking for so many people, Lord.*

"Did you need me to escort you to the bunkhouse, Miss?" A man with rusty-colored hair stood beside her, his fingers wrapping around the brim of the hat in his hands. He jutted an elbow.

"That would be wonderful. Thank you, Mr., uh...?" She slipped her hand through the crook.

"No mister. Just Russ." Color filled his tanned face.

The door to the bunkhouse slammed open, smoke pouring from inside.

"Fire!" One of the cowboys bellowed. "Get buckets and start filling them, fellas."

Noah staggered from the building, doubled over, coughing and hacking.

Her heart quickened. She released the arm of the cowboy escorting her, lifted her skirt, and sprinted toward Noah.

Chaos sounded behind her as men shouted orders to each other. Their boots clomping against the frozen prairie grass.

Her breathing came in quick gasps as she reached Noah. "We." She took a choppy breath. "Need to get." Another breath. "You... out of here." Kitty pulled on Noah's arm.

He hacked and waved his hand from side to side. "No need."

Clearly, the smoke had addled his brain.

She didn't wait for him to say anything more, dragging him toward safety. Kitty didn't stop leading him until they reached the sprawling ranch house. "Here, sit on the steps until you catch your breath."

He collapsed on the bottom step, still coughing.

"I'll be right back." Normally Kitty wouldn't barge into the house without being asked, but she refused to stand idly by while Noah suffered. She may not care for him, but she wouldn't want even an enemy to undergo pain.

Unsure where to go once she'd stepped inside the house, Kitty passed through a sitting room on her right and a dining room on the left. She opted for the small hallway, hoping it led to the kitchen.

Sure enough. Once in the tidy room, Kitty spotted a pitcher. Crossing the room, she discovered it filled with water. She opened cupboard doors until she found one with glasses in it. Snagging one, she poured the water into it and scurried back the way she'd came.

Outside again, she pressed the glass into Noah's outstretched hand. "Here, drink this."

He took a long swallow, finishing it in a matter of seconds. "Thank you."

Another cough racked his chest.

"I'll get you some more."

Noah shook his head. "No. I'll be fine."

"Are you sure?" She stooped down beside him. "It's no trouble to refill it for you."

"I'm sure." He handed her the glass.

The warmth of his fingers grazed the exposed portion of her wrist, between the top of her gloves and the bottom sleeve of her coat. A spark shimmied up her arm, nearly causing her to drop the glass. Kitty shook her head. Nothing like that had ever happened before.

"Something wrong?" His hazel-eyed gaze about did Kitty in.

What was happening? If she didn't know better, she would've thought she'd been exposed to the smoke instead of him. It made no sense.

"Kitty?" His eyes filled with concern.

She shook her head, trying to clear away the nonsense. There's no way she'd ever develop feelings for him. His near accident merely left her discombobulated.

Commotion at the bunkhouse snagged her attention.

Men guffawed as one carried a big smoking pot of something. She could smell the scorchness of whatever had been cooking from here. "What on earth?" Kitty's gaze bounced to Noah.

His eyes widened, and he ducked his head.

Maybe something was wrong with him even though he denied it before. She bit her lip trying to discern what to do. Should she go over and see what the men had discovered, or should she stay with Noah in case he needed her assistance again?

The group of fellas headed toward them.

Thank You, Lord. Maybe they'll be able to make some sense of what's happening here. If anything, they'll be able to take care of Noah better than I can.

Noah lapped up Kitty's unexpected attention like a neglected dog starving for attention... until one of his men popped out of the bunkhouse with the smoking frying pan.

"Found the cause of the smoke, boss."

Oh no. Would Kitty continue to lavish her concerned care on him when she found out the truth?

All his hands gathered around the pan and pot, staring at them, before doubling over with guffaws.

Great. Just what I need.

"Good thing you hired Miss Love, boss." Shorty's brown eyes twinkled.

"I don't understand." A frown furrowed on Kitty's brow.

"Why are you being so insensitive toward Noah?"

He coughed, not from the smoke he'd inhaled but uncomfortable about how she'd feel about him once she heard the truth of what happened. Noah couldn't help shifting on the step.

Russ chortled. "Glad Miss Love arrived before you finished the meal."

Kitty planted her fists on her slim hips. "I'm beginning to think twice about cooking for the lot of you when you behave like this. You'd think you'd show more respect to Mr. Eldridge."

Shorty hurried over to her, gripping Kitty's hand. "We're sorry, Miss Love. Please don't leave us." He motioned toward the still-smoking frying pan. "You can see the boss can't cook worth a lick." He scrubbed a hand through his dark beard. "Truth is... I'm not any better."

Her right eyebrow quirked. "You mean all the smoke came from your cooking?" She narrowed her eyes.

Noah rolled his gaze heavenward. Looked like there was no use denying it. He gave a tight nod.

"What on earth were you cooking to cause so much smoke?" Her lower lip gaped open.

He cleared his throat. "Umm, bacon."

"But to get it to burn and smoke like that, it must've been on extremely high heat, and you had to have cooked it to a crisp." She strolled over to where Bull held the frying pan. "Oh, dear. None of you really know how to cook, do you?"

So, she wasn't mad at him?

"Truth is, we haven't had a decent meal since our cookie left over a month ago when he got word his ma was ailing and sent for him." Henry leaned against the railing of the steps. "No offense, Shorty."

"None taken."

Kitty's gaze crashed into Noah's. "But why were you cooking when you asked me to do it?"

It felt like a branding iron seared his cheeks. "Well… knowing our history…"

"You were afraid I wouldn't come." She finished his thoughts, shaking her head. "If you had ever taken the time to get to know me in school, you would've learned that I follow through when I make a commitment."

He deserved her reprimand… and so much more than that too. "I'm sorry about the—"

"Where's she going to cook now?" Bull set the frying pan on the ground. "It smells to high heaven in the bunkhouse. No place for a fine woman like Miss Love."

Shorty nodded. "He's right, boss. Even with airing out the place until bedtime, it's going to stink for a while."

"I don't see any reason why I can't cook in your kitchen, Noah." She rested a hand on his sleeve.

When she batted her eyelashes like that, a man could barely think straight. Was she trying to flirt with him, or had she gotten a speck of dirt in her eye? Of course, then again, the smoke probably hadn't helped either. So much for trying to impress Kitty. She'd likely only been nice to him more so as concern for his welfare, like she would've been for anybody else. *Don't take it personally, Eldridge, or you're going to get hurt. Buck up.*

"Don't seem right for the little lady to cook in the bunkhouse with the windows open." Trusty peeked at Kitty before averting his gaze. "It'll be too cold for the likes of her."

"Of course not. You're welcome to head into the kitchen, Kitty."

She puffed out a breath, sending a curl that had slipped from her loose bun, bouncing against her forehead.

Noah couldn't help wondering if it would be soft between his fingers.

"You feelin' alright, boss?" Trusty edged closer. "You're actin' mighty strange-like."

The last thing he needed was for his men to learn of his infatuation with Kitty. He'd never hear the end of it, if they did. "I guess inhaling the smoke from all the bacon grease has rattled my head for a bit... but I'll be just fine." He stood, holding on to the railing for a second as his vision blurred for a second.

"Maybe one of you should ride into town and get the doc." Henry rubbed his chin, a twinkle in his eye.

"Told you I'm fine." He motioned to the men. "It's about time you fellas got back to work. One of you should air out the bunkhouse, and the rest of you check on the herd. Kitt... er... Miss Love will call you when the chow's ready."

The men glanced at him for a second before dispersing.

Noah breathed easier once they left for their respective jobs.

Henry waggled his eyebrows. "Did you want me to show Miss Love the kitchen while you rest for a while?"

There was no telling what his foreman would share with Kitty if he got her alone. The man knew far too much about how Noah had pined for her through the years.

"Why don't you work on the books?"

Henry's brow rose even higher.

The financial part of the ranch was typically something he took care of. The crazy man had Noah rattled even to suggest it.

"Whatever you say, boss." He grinned and headed up the steps to the ranch house.

"I'm sure I'll be able to figure things out for myself." Kitty lifted her split-skirt a smidgen as she took to the stairs. "I wouldn't want you overdoing it."

Noah could be bleeding or hurting something awful, and he'd still do whatever he could to spend more time with her. Now if only he could tell her that.

CHAPTER FOUR

K itty needed to get a hold of herself. She didn't know what had come over her when she'd seen Noah staggering from the smoky bunkhouse. It wasn't like she cared about the man. If anything, her feelings were far from it. She wouldn't want anyone to be injured. Shaking her head, she followed Noah as he led the way to the kitchen that she'd been in minutes earlier.

"I don't think you've ever been to the house before." Noah's cheeks filled with color. More than likely embarrassed by the contentious relationship they'd had through the years.

Or at least, Kitty hoped he regretted how he'd treated her when they were in school. *Enough. It's time to set it aside and not let him know how much he hurt me.* Tears pricked her eyes as some of those memories flooded back.

"... and the dry goods are over here." He lifted a long length of fabric, revealing a small pantry.

What else had she missed while ruminating about the

past? Kitty shook her head. No matter. It wouldn't take her long to learn where everything was located. She glanced at the cuckoo clock as it sounded from the far wall. "With it being so late, perhaps it's best if I fix a quick meal. How many men did you say work here?"

"Don't think I did. Counting me and Henry, my foreman, there's eleven of us currently. It can fluctuate throughout the year."

"So many. I never knew you had a big enough spread to need that many cowboys." She tugged a frying pan from a hook, placing it on the cookstove. "I see eggs, but do you have any bacon?"

His face and neck turned ruddy again. "Er... there's some in the root cellar. I'll go get it for you."

"Are you sure you're feeling up to it?" She touched his sleeve. "I haven't heard you cough in a while. If you tell me where it is, I can do it."

He shook his head. "No, I'll go." Noah scurried out the back door before she could respond.

"Well, I guess it's just me then."

Kitty tugged open cupboards and drawers until she found what she needed to make a simple lunch of fried eggs and bacon. She also whipped up a quick batch of fry bread. Hopefully, it would be enough to tide the cowboys over until she could make a more rib-sticking supper.

She tied an apron around her waist. Scooping flour into a bowl, she added baking powder and a pinch of salt, mixing it together with her fingers. Satisfied it was the right consistency, Kitty dusted her hands on a towel. She shifted a pan to a hotter part of the stovetop, the lard sizzling as she flattened the fry bread and lightly pressed it into the pan.

"Here you go." Noah plunked a side of bacon onto the table. "I'll be at the barn if you need me."

She didn't bother to answer, keeping an eye on the bread. Satisfied it wouldn't burn, Kitty grabbed a knife and sliced the bacon, dropping it into the second frying pan. In the third pan, butter sputtered as she cracked eggs into it.

With years of practice, Kitty monitored each of the pans, flipping fry bread, eggs, and bacon as needed. Reaching for a platter, she soon had an overflowing stack of food. "I wonder if it'll be enough to feed them all. I'm not used to making for so many at one time."

"Did you say something, Miss Love?" Henry Kierman leaned against the doorway to the kitchen. "Mmm. Thought I smelled something good. The fellas are going to be mighty happy."

She wiped a hand across her perspired forehead. "I'm not sure if I made enough. I have only a few that I usually feed."

"Well, it might not be quite enough. The men haven't been having any good meals lately."

"I suppose you could call them, and they could get started on what I have so far." Kitty forked some more bacon onto the platter. "I can keep making more, but I'm not sure whether they'll eat in the bunkhouse, here, or am I to figure that out too?" She darted a glance at the foreman.

He shook his head. "Don't you worry about it, Miss Love. I'll get some of the hands to fetch plates from the bunkhouse."

"Thank you."

Henry set his Stetson in place. "Be right back, Miss."

Kitty removed the fry bread, scooping a little more lard into the hot pan. It popped and spat onto her hand. She sucked in a breath, wiping the back of her hand on the apron, before adding more fry bread to the pan.

She kept focused on flipping bacon, cracking more eggs into the other pan, and shifting the fry bread as the food cooked. It didn't take long to fill another platter.

The scrape of boots on the wooden floor drew her attention to the doorway. Noah held his brown Stetson in his hands. "I guess for now, we'll have the men come in and fill their plates. The bunkhouse is still too smoky for them to eat in there. If we squeeze in tight, we should be able to fit around the dining room table."

She gave a brief nod. "Whatever you think is best, unless you'd rather I bring the platters. Oh no, I just realized something."

"What is it?" Noah took a few steps into the room. "Is there something you need?"

She flipped her hand toward the cupboard. "I forgot to start some coffee."

He shifted closer to her. "What happened to your hand?"

Kitty chuckled. "Nothing more than normal, the hot oil spattered." Before she knew it, Noah gripped her hand in his.

"We should get some butter on this to take the sting out." His hazel eyes filled with emotion.

Kitty couldn't identify it.

Her pulse sped up a bit as he continued to hold her hand. *What is wrong with me, Lord? It's not like he has any feelings for me... nor do I want him to. Maybe the smoke has gotten to me too.*

"Does this mean you're staking a claim on the little filly, boss?"

Kitty's heart skipped a beat as a tall cowboy strolled toward them.

Of all the rotten timing, why did Beau decide to step into the room just then? Noah was regretting his most recent hire with the way Kitty fluttered her eyelashes as she studied the tall man. The last thing Noah needed was for her to fall for someone other than himself.

"Nobody has staked a claim on me yet." Her cheeks pinked as she licked her lips. "Least of all Noah." Kitty tugged her hand free from his grip. She giggled.

Way to make a fella feel lower than dirt.

Beau removed his Stetson. A brown wavy lock of hair fell onto his broad forehead as he took Kitty's hand in his, kissing the back of it.

Good grief. Surely Kitty wouldn't fall for the man's antics, would she?

"I don't think we've met before." The cowboy winked at Kitty. "I'm Beau."

"Kitty Love." She dipped her head for a second before a smile tugged at her cheeks. "It's a pleasure to meet you, Mr. Beau."

"All my friends just call me Beau, and I hope we'll be good friends, Miss Love." He waggled his eyebrows at her.

Noah needed to put a stop to this. He picked up a platter, shoving it into Beau's other hand. "Here, take this into the dining room."

"Yes, boss." Beau balanced it while also planting another kiss on Kitty's hand, which he had yet to release.

"I thought you wanted the men to fill their plates here." She finally tugged her hand free from the cowboy's grip.

He folded his arms across his chest. "Changed my mind."

"There's no reason to be crotchety. You're acting like a bear with its paw caught in a trap."

Noah forced himself to bank his simmering embers. He'd deal with the brazen cowboy after lunch. "I'm sorry, Kitty. What else needs done to get the food on the table?"

She turned her attention back to the stove. "I think everything is about ready other than not having coffee. I can start some, but it won't be ready for a while."

"No need. We always keep a big pot going in the bunkhouse. I'll have one of the fellas fetch it." And he knew just the one he wanted out of the way for a few minutes.

"Oh good. Next time, I'll be sure to have a pot going as well." She handed him a platter. "Would you mind taking this to the table?"

As he accepted it from her, her fingers slid across his.

His heart pounded in his chest.

One shapely eyebrow lifted as she watched him. "Are you sure you're feeling alright?"

He gave a nod before leaving the room.

Henry lounged on the other side of the doorframe. He shifted closer, whispering. "If you ask me, you'd better monitor our new cowpoke, or you may find him snatching

Kitty up before you get the chance to tell her how you feel about her."

Noah bit back a moan. The last thing he needed was competition for Kitty's affections.

Kitty ran a hand through her hair, tucking stray locks back into her loose bun. *Who'd have thought You'd be so quick to bring a new man into my life, Lord? Maybe assisting Noah will end up helping me as well.* She refrained from chuckling. Instead, she smoothed her apron as she carried the last platter into the dining room.

Chairs scraped the floor as the men stood.

"I saved a seat for you here, Miss Love." Beau winked as he ran a hand along his mustache.

Noah frowned from his place at the head of the table.

She couldn't imagine what had gotten his hackles raised. "Please have a seat." Kitty motioned to the men, but they still remained standing until Beau tugged the chair out for her. She slipped into the seat without another word.

"Let's pray." Noah bowed his head, and the rest of the cowboys followed suit.

She dipped her head as well, pleased to see the men respond in such a way.

"Father, we thank You for this day. For protecting uh... that is..."

Kitty couldn't help peeking at Beau and Noah for a second before squeezing her eyes shut again.

"Thank You for Kitty's willingness to come and be our cook until I find someone to take her place. Bless this food, Kitty, and her hands that capably prepared it. I'm uh... er... we're blessed to have her here. Amen."

The men echoed the end of Noah's prayer.

She darted a glance at the head of the table. None of her family had ever mentioned being blessed to have her. At least not in words. She knew they loved her and appreciated what she did, but to have someone actually mention it.

"I, for one, am glad you're here." Beau winked at her again, setting her pulse to stuttering in her veins.

"I'm Shorty, Miss." A man smiled at her from the chair on her other side. "You're taking over for me, and I couldn't be more thankful. I can't wait to get back in the saddle again instead of stuck cooking."

"I don't think we can call what you did cooking, Shorty." Russ's mustache twitched.

The men guffawed as their eyes twinkled.

Kitty dished food onto her plate before passing the platter. "I recognize some of you, but if you could tell me your names, I'd appreciate the reminder."

She struggled to keep track of the names as the men introduced themselves. "Let me see if I got this straight." She pointed to each one. "Shorty, Russ, Carson, Trusty, Henry, and of course Noah I've known all my life." Kitty squinted one eye shut as she glanced at the man beside Noah. "Let's see, Morgan, Sherman, Colt, Bull, and Beau."

"You've got it, Miss Love." Shorty cackled beside her.

"If I'm going to be here every day for a while, you might as well call me Kitty." She bit off a piece of fry bread, dipping it into her runny egg yolk.

"I don't know if that's a good idea." Noah had that odd look again.

What was up with him? It made little sense?

CHAPTER FIVE

February 5, 1877

"A re you sure we can't let Beau go?" Noah thrust his fingers through his hair.

A chuckle rumbled from Henry's chest. "Why is the fella such a burr in your hide?"

He scowled at his foreman. "You know why." Ever since Kitty's first day on the job a couple weeks ago, Beau had gone out of his way to charm her, and it seemed to be working.

"Between Shorty still healing and three of the men down with the ague and a couple others feeling poorly, we need all the help with moving the cattle to that second winter pasture. Never thought we'd have a warm spell for so long."

"Every time I turn around, Beau's finding some excuse to spend time with Kitty." Noah bit back a growl. His foreman didn't need Noah taking his frustration out on him. "Maybe I should ban all of the men from talking with her."

"As if that would go over well." Henry shifted in the

saddle, glancing to where the men were corralling the longhorns.

Too bad Beau wasn't one of the men who'd taken sick. Noah's conscience immediately pricked. *Forgive me, Lord. I know better than to wish someone to be ill. Could You give me some ideas of how to get her to take an interest in me?* His grip tightened on the reins. *Or is this Your way of trying to get it through my thick skull that Kitty isn't the gal You've picked for me?*

Noah's stallion shook his head.

"Sorry, boy." He leaned forward to pat the wide side of the horse's neck.

Beau rode toward them. "I think we have all the cattle in the new pasture, boss. Did you have anything else you wanted us to do before we head in for supper?" He studied the sky. "It'll be dark soon."

Noah couldn't help shooting a sideways look at Henry. "We might as well head in." He turned his horse toward home.

Beau, Bull, and Colt urged their mounts, passing up Noah and Henry.

"If anything, the fellas are happy with Kitty's cooking." His foreman's eyes sparkled. "At least one of your problems is solved. The men aren't talking about leaving anymore."

"Nobody could complain about her meals." Noah patted his stomach. "I think I've gained a few pounds since she started."

Henry's lips twitched. "No doubt all of us have. She definitely will make a fine catch for someone, if you know what I mean."

Noah scowled at his friend. "And how do you

recommend I go about that?"

"Tell her how you really feel. Apologize for the past. Let her know you only acted like you did on account of caring for her."

He made it sound easy.

"Since you've had her keep on cooking in the house instead of the bunkhouse, you should have plenty of opportunities to speak with her. Maybe make a point of asking her to the sweetheart dance next week." Henry waggled his eyebrows.

The man was incorrigible.

"Do you think she'd go with me?"

"You won't know until you ask her." Henry's eyes softened. "I'll be praying for you."

"I appreciate it." It'd be a lot easier asking Kitty if he knew she'd respond favorably.

"I think I'll go check on the sick men first." Henry motioned toward the house as they brought their horses to a stop. "You should head on into the house while you have the chance." He didn't bother to wait for Noah's response, instead, he tied his horse to the hitching post and strode toward the bunkhouse.

Noah swung down from his mount, tugging the reins as he led the stallion to the barn. It wouldn't hurt to get some gumption up and get in some prayers while he took care of his horse.

The rhythmic brushing of his steed helped to calm Noah's agitation. *Lord, You know what's best. But I can't help asking for Kitty to give a favorable response to my question. Could You straighten the way for me?*

He chucked the brush into the wooden box and rubbed his horse between the ears. "Well, I guess it's now or never."

The barn door creaked as he closed it behind him.

Noah set his hat on a fencepost before traipsing to the water pump, lifting the handle up and down until a steady stream flowed. He thrust his hand into the cold water, took a sip of the liquid, and then slicked his hair back. Before he lost his nerve, Noah shoved the Stetson back in place.

With a prayer, he opened the front door.

The soft murmur of voices came from the kitchen.

Had someone come to visit Kitty while she prepared the evening meal?

As he drew closer to the kitchen, Noah recognized the voice.

Beau.

I knew I should've assigned him something to do when he got back.

Noah hesitated a few feet away from the doorway.

The scent of chicken caused his gut to growl.

"The fellas were talking about a dance coming up next week." Beau's deep voice could be easily heard from the hallway.

"You're talking about the sweetheart dance." Kitty sounded breathless. Like she'd been running.

Noah had never heard her talk like that before.

"Does everyone have to bring a sweetheart to attend?"

Kitty giggled. "No. Everybody goes to it. It's a chance to get together as a community and to do something fun during the winter months. My sisters and I have gone every year since I can remember." Her voice softened. "Although

I guess they'll be going with their husbands this time."

Noah needed to get in there. He hurried into the room, frowning at Beau before turning to Kitty. "I wanted to ask you something, Kitty."

Her cheeks were bright, like the sky before the sun made an appearance.

Beau shifted closer to Kitty, snagging her hand. "I would love for you to do the honor of going with me to the sweetheart dance." He winked at her. "I'd hate for you not to have anyone to be with this time."

She held a hand to her chest. "I'd love to, Beau."

They exchanged tender glances before she shifted her gaze to Noah. "What did you want to ask me, Noah?"

Kitty could hardly contain her excitement as she swung down from the saddle, flipping the reins over the hitching post in front of Teddy and Paul's home.

The front door opened, and her new brother-in-law stepped onto the porch. "Kitty? Is something wrong?"

Teddy poked her head out before joining her husband. "What's goin' on? Thought you'd be home by now. It's pert near dark."

She rushed up the steps. "I just had to see you, Teddy."

Paul's eyes widened. "Sounds like some girl talk I don't need to be part of." He kissed his wife's cheek. "I'll be in the barn if you need me."

"You'll never guess what happened." Kitty squealed and

grabbed her sister's arm, tugging her into the house.

"What's all the fuss about?" Teddy motioned to the kitchen table. "Have a seat."

"One of Noah's men asked me to the dance next week." She perched on the edge of a straight-backed chair.

"What's his name? Would I know him?"

She shook her head. "I don't think so. I'm pretty sure he's fairly new to the area. His name is Beau."

"Does he have a last name?"

Kitty puzzled over the question for a few seconds. "Come to think of it, I don't know the last names of most of Noah's men. They introduced themselves only with their given name or some kind of nickname."

"What do you know about this Beau?" Teddy flipped her waist-length braid over her shoulder as she straddled a chair. "Is he a new hire? Don't reckon I've heard the name before."

She shrugged. "I'm not sure how long he's been with the ranch. That hasn't ever come up, but he has the most beautiful wavy brown hair."

Teddy snorted. "How a man looks has no bearin' on how he'd be treatin' you or if he serves the Almighty."

"Of course, but to be asked to the dance." Kitty held a hand to her chest. "It's so romantic, don't you think?"

Her younger sister rolled her eyes. "You always were the dramatic one of the three of us."

"You have to admit, now that you're married, love and courtship have their place." After all, Teddy had snagged their neighbor's interest.

Her sister ducked her head as her cheeks turned crimson.

Kitty's mouth gaped open. She didn't think she'd ever seen that kind of reaction from Teddy up until now.

"I just don't want you fallin' for the first fella to show interest in you. Have you prayed about Beau?"

This time it was Kitty's turn to have her cheeks feel like they were on fire. "Not exactly. But he's been so sweet to me. He always makes a point of talking to me each day and complimenting my cooking."

"I'd reckon most of Noah's men do that."

She took a second to consider Teddy's words. "True... but..."

"If you ask me, you're tryin' to convince yourself it's a good thing this fella asked you to the dance."

Tears pricked Kitty's eyes as she jumped to her feet. "I came here thinking you'd be happy for me instead of finding fault with Beau." She wiped the tears that streaked her cheeks. "You and Essie already each have husbands. Why can't you be excited for me since I finally have a man interested in me and not just for my cooking ability?"

"Now, Kitty, that's not what I meant, and you know it. Don't be so touchy." Teddy put her hands out as if she were trying to calm down a startled horse.

She didn't wait for her sister to say anything else. Instead, Kitty scurried to the door and flung it open. She ran down the steps and mounted the mare before Teddy made it to the porch.

"Wait, Kitty. Don't go off like this. I didn't mean to—"

She kicked her mount into motion, not waiting for Teddy to say anything else. Kitty didn't look back as she urged the horse to a gallop.

Once she got out of sight of Paul and Teddy's home, Kitty slowed the mare. Even with being upset, she knew it was foolhardy to race the horse when only the light of the moon guided her.

The short distance to home passed way too quickly. She hadn't fully composed her emotions before she reached the barn.

Jud met her, helping her down from the horse. "Essie and I were getting concerned something had happened to you. You've never been this late before."

Kitty was thankful for the darkness, and that her brother-in-law likely hadn't glimpsed her wet cheeks. "I'm fine. Just made a quick stop to see Teddy."

"How're they doing?" Jud slipped the reins over the mare's head, leading her inside the barn, where a single lantern lit the area.

She stayed in the shadows, wiping her cheeks while Jud had his back to her. "I stayed only a few minutes."

He turned toward her. "Are you sure you're alright?"

She gave a brief nod. "I had best get inside." Not waiting for Jud's response, she slipped away. Her stomach rumbled as she strolled along the dirt path to the front door. Taking a deep breath, Kitty pasted on what would pass as a smile as she went inside.

Essie patted Miriam's back, then resumed stirring something on the cookstove.

"Mmm. Smells good. What did you make?" She took a step closer, peering into the pot.

"Corn chowder. Are you hungry, or did you eat at the ranch?" Her gaze swung to meet Kitty's. "What's wrong? Did you get injured on the way home? I knew we shouldn't have let you travel back and forth to the ranch on your own." She set the baby in the nearby cradle before swallowing Kitty in a hug before setting her at arm's length. Essie's gaze traveled the length of Kitty's frame as if assessing for injuries.

Her throat tightened as the conversation with Teddy flooded back. What was the likelihood of Essie coming up with the same thoughts?

CHAPTER SIX

K itty spent the night tossing and turning. She didn't enjoy being at odds with her sisters. Unfortunately, the conversation with Essie had gone about as well as the one with Teddy. If Kitty hadn't known better, she would've guessed they'd discussed the matter before she'd even told them about Beau.

She shoved back the covers. Might as well face the day. Yawning as she tugged off her nightgown, Kitty shivered as she removed her clothes from the hook. As she lit the lantern, she could see her breath as she fastened the bodice of her green wool dress.

Too bad working at the ranch wouldn't allow her the time needed to sew a new dress for the upcoming dance. Oh well. At least she could wear one Beau hadn't seen before. Brushing her below-waist hair took only a matter of minutes before she pinned it in a loose chignon. Kitty glanced in the mirror before tugging a few tendrils of hair from the bun to create curls at the side of her face.

Her heart fluttered as she examined her reflection one last time. Would Beau notice the difference?

She blew out the light before opening the door to her room. Kitty tiptoed across the kitchen, struggling to see in the darkness. She quickly shrugged into her coat, trying not to awaken her sister and her little family. The thought was a reminder of what Kitty longed for.

With a sigh, she closed the door behind her.

The moon still shone as she hurried to the barn.

Maybe I should've checked the clock to see what time it is. She shrugged her shoulders. It made little difference. If anything, once at the ranch, she could prepare meals for the entire day and maybe ask Noah if he minded if she left a little earlier than normal. At some point, Kitty would have to apologize to Teddy and Essie. Although she couldn't help feeling her sisters needed to do some type of asking forgiveness too.

I'm sorry, Lord. I know that You tell us to forgive, and it's not contingent on the other person. The words of her prayer felt as if they'd poked a hole in her heart. Her eyes widened as she slipped the saddle onto the mare. Had she ever fully forgiven Noah for all his pranks through their school years? She squirmed, not wanting to examine the topic any further. Shoving the thought aside, she tightened the strap around the girth of the mare.

Minutes later, she led the horse outside, closing the barn door. Swinging up onto the saddle, she turned the mount toward the LazE Spur Ranch. Kitty set her mind on the food Noah had on hand and what meals she'd create for the day. Maybe she'd make several batches of cookies for the men to enjoy. What kind did Beau like?

The miles passed, and before she knew it, she'd arrived at the ranch. Darkness still filled the sky. Not even the pre-light of dawn shimmered on the horizon. She swung down, wrapping the reins around the hitching post. Patting the mare's muzzle, she murmured. "I'll have one of the hands take care of you once they're up and moving."

She crept up the steps, cringing as one stair creaked. Kitty halted for a minute, holding her breath. When no sound came from the house, she climbed the last steps, opening the front door.

Darkness filled the house as Kitty felt her way to the kitchen doorway. *Now, where did I put the lantern before leaving yesterday?* She shifted forward only to run into a corner of the table, bumping her hip hard against it. The loud screech of the table leg against the wooden floor reverberated through the room.

Her heart pattered as she fumbled to strike a match.

She squealed when she turned to see Noah pointing a gun at her.

"Kitty? Is that you?" He lowered the weapon. "What're you doing here in the middle of the night?"

His brown hair stood on end. One strap of his suspenders draped around the waist of his trousers, with the other over a very muscular shoulder. The outline was clearly visible under his tight union suit stretching across his upper torso.

She quickly averted her gaze and lit the lantern before the flame from the match burned her fingertips. "I couldn't sleep, so I thought maybe to start a little earlier than usual."

"Early? You do know it's three in the morning, don't you?"

His words caused her to cast a tentative glance at Noah. A whole heap of emotions tangled in his eyes.

It made no sense that her pulse stuttered in her veins. Kitty couldn't ever consider him as more than her employer and the person who had made her life miserable for a good portion of her childhood. "Three? Are you sure?"

She glanced at the cuckoo clock. Sure enough. It was just a few minutes after the hour.

Heat sprang to her cheeks. "I'm so sorry. I should've checked the time before I headed here." She wouldn't make *that* mistake again.

What would his men think of them if they found the two of them alone together?

The side door to the kitchen screeched open. "Everything alright in here?" Henry stepped into the room, glancing back and forth between Noah and Kitty.

"It isn't the way it looks..." Kitty raised a hand to try to alleviate the heat of the fire creeping into her cheeks.

Henry smiled, leaning against the doorframe.

Noah growled. "Nothing happened... she just arrived... I wouldn't." He set the rifle in the corner.

The foreman's eyes sparkled. "I heard her horse a few minutes ago. Thought I'd come investigate."

"I didn't know the time." Mist filled her eyes. Could it get any worse?

"Something going on here?"

Kitty looked in horror as Shorty and Beau shoved inside the kitchen. She wanted to hide her face or find some corner to crawl into where nobody could see her.

"And here I thought you had no claim on her." A scowl

marred Beau's face. "I see the way it is. But at least she's agreed to go with me to the dance."

Noah snapped his other suspender in place on his shoulder. He scrubbed his hand along his jaw. "Kitty, er, Miss Love, didn't realize the time and arrived a little earlier than normal." He shot a look at Henry.

"The boss is right. Miss Love only arrived a few minutes ago." Henry nodded to the men. "It's best if you two head back to the bunkhouse."

"As long as there's nothing wrong, I'm going back to bed." Shorty yawned, tipping his hat as he left.

Beau lifted a dark eyebrow as he ran his fingers through his thick wavy hair. "I'll have to take your word for it." His gaze entangled with Kitty's. "I don't have any plans of intertwining myself with a woman of loose morals."

Kitty sucked in a breath, tears pricking her eyes.

Noah curled his fingers to keep himself from slugging Beau. How dare the man insinuate such horrible things about Kitty? "Miss Love is one of the finest women I've ever known, and I demand you apologize to her immediately."

He took a step closer to her.

While he longed to wrap an arm around her shoulders to protect her, Noah recognized it would only muddy the stream.

Kitty's chin wobbled before she stood a little taller. "If that's the way you feel, maybe it's best if we don't go to the dance together next week. I couldn't bear to go to the event with someone who questioned my morality."

"I just wanted to make my intention known of desiring a pure woman."

Noah shot a glance at Kitty. It didn't look like she was convinced. He couldn't help being a little relieved at the change of events. No sooner had the thought crossed his mind when he cast it aside. *Forgive me, Lord.*

"I would *never* do something like that." Kitty's hands fluttered at her side. "I only got mixed up on the time." She shook her head. "Noah would never interest me."

Way to deflate a man's ego. So much for thinking she'd ever care about me. Noah bit back his disappointment.

Beau didn't respond, just stared hard at Kitty before turning his back and leaving.

Henry cleared his throat.

Noah dragged his attention to his friend.

"As much as I'd love to get some more shuteye, it might be best if I stay here to chaperone you two." His foreman grabbed a chair, settling himself into it.

"I'm really sorry, Noah... Mr. Kierman." She wiped the tears from her cheeks. "I should never have come. Maybe it's best if I go back home and come back later."

Noah checked the clock. "That makes little sense. You'd no sooner get home than you'd have to leave to come again before long." He caught Kitty's gaze. "I'll squelch any rumors with my men."

Her lower lip trembled. "T-thank you."

It took everything in him to keep from taking her into her arms and soothing her raw emotions.

Henry stood, closing the distance, handing Kitty a handkerchief. "Here you go, Miss Love."

She sniffed, wiping her tears.

His foreman awkwardly patted Kitty's shoulder. "Don't you worry, Miss. We'll take care of the fellas."

"I appreciate it."

Henry waggled his eyebrows as his eyes cut in Noah's direction. "Maybe you should finish getting dressed."

Blistering heat coursed up Noah's neck and into his face. He refrained from folding his arms across his chest to hide the tight material of his union suit. "I'll be back." He snagged the rifle as he quickly exited the kitchen.

He scurried to his bedroom, placing the rifle on a holder on the wall. Not bothering to light a lamp, Noah found his shirt hanging from the end bedpost. He shrugged into it, fastening the buttons, before shoving the shirt into the waist of his pants. After running his fingers through his hair, he snagged his Stetson, setting it in place.

Noah started down the hallway, planning on entering the kitchen when Henry's words halted him.

"You know he's always had a hankering for you."

He slapped his hand against his forehead. Could the day get any worse?

Noah couldn't resist creeping closer to the doorway of the kitchen. He hid in the shadows, still able to see what Henry and Kitty were doing without them spotting him. Or, at least, he hoped so.

Kitty's mouth gaped open. Had she really heard what she'd thought the foreman had said? She shook her head. Surely, Henry was mistaken. Noah had shown no inclination towards her. If anything, the opposite. "Why would you say something like that? Noah has shown only contempt for me." She turned her back, opening a cupboard, and removing a big mixing bowl.

"I reckon you have little experience with little boys or brothers." A twinkle shimmered in the man's eyes. "I was in the middle of my four brothers. Had no sisters, so I can't attest to how they think and act."

She lifted the container of flour from the shelf, placing it beside the various tins of spices. "My sisters never acted or treated me like Noah did."

Henry nodded. "I thought as much. When you were in school, did you notice the fellas teasing other boys?"

Kitty measured flour into the bowl before responding. "They were often rough and got into trouble for their shenanigans. Sometimes playing pranks on each other."

"Even though Noah had no siblings, he was no different." Henry chuckled. "He was always playing one prank or another on the men."

"Really? Why would he do that?" She wiped her hands on the apron tied around her waist.

"Because that's what fellas do when they care about somebody. I guess they don't know how to deal with emotions, so instead of saying something, they might slug another fella in the arm. Or if it's a gal, he might put a frog in a lunch pail, or some other sort of mischief." Henry sent her a pointed look.

She considered his words for a few minutes before her pulse skittered. "But... if that's true, it means..." Kitty couldn't finish her sentence. Was Henry trying to imply Noah had always held special feelings for her and not contempt?

Chapter Seven

February 14, 1877

K itty smoothed the skirt of her deep blue wool dress. The one she kept for special occasions. With all that had transpired at the LazE Spur Ranch the past week, she'd told Beau it was best if he just met her at the church. Even though he'd tried to apologize for his harsh words when she'd ended up at the ranch well before her normal starting time, they still stung.

And after her conversation with Henry, Kitty hadn't known what to think of Noah. Or what to think about their troubled past. She also couldn't help wondering what he'd wanted to ask her before Beau had invited her to the dance.

She blew out a breath. All this wondering wouldn't get her anywhere.

"There you are." Teddy bustled toward her. "Seems like you've been avoidin' me."

Truth be told, Kitty had been steering clear of both of her sisters. It hadn't been an easy task either, when she lived with one of them.

Maybe changing the topic would help to circumvent questioning. "You look really pretty, Teddy. Is that a new dress?" Kitty knew her youngest sister rarely wore one.

Teddy pinched the material of her burgundy dress. "Paul bought it for me. Figured it'd be appropriate for the sweetheart dance on account of it bein' red."

"I like it." Kitty pulled her sister into a quick hug. "I'm sorry for how I acted earlier last week."

"Wasn't all your fault." Teddy's broad forehead wrinkled. "You know I've always been one to say things and not hold back. I didn't mean to hurt you. Just concerned about you rushin' into somethin' head long without first considerin' things."

"I know."

"There you two are." Essie hurried over, the baby cradled in her arms. "I've been looking all over for you. I thought you were going to ride with us, Kitty."

She had needed the time to think, so she'd walked the mile to town. Fortunately, the snow from earlier in the week had melted enough to make the path easy to traipse through.

Kitty reached for Miriam, patting her small back when she fussed. "Let me hold my niece. I haven't seen much of her lately." She immediately regretted her words as her older sister pierced her with a stare.

"And why is it you've been avoiding us?"

How could she share what transpired when she'd arrived at the ranch in the middle of the night? If her sisters learned of it, they'd demand she marry Noah to save her reputation.

Thankfully, the ranch hands hadn't seemed to spread the information anywhere. Noah had been good about keeping his word.

"Excuse me, ladies, but I believe Miss Love has promised me this next dance." Beau bowed, reaching for her hand.

Kitty handed the baby back to Essie.

Both of her sisters stood with their wide brows wrinkling as Beau led her to the makeshift dance floor. The pews of the church had been shifted to the sides of the room. Music swelled as couples swirled.

"I wasn't sure if you'd show, Kitty." He clasped her hand tighter. "I'm glad you've forgiven me for the misunderstanding."

She bristled. His words certainly hadn't been a miscommunication. If anything, maybe Beau's true character had been on display.

Maybe Kitty's sisters were right. She didn't exactly know much about Beau or where he came from, come to think of it. It was time she remedied that. "I don't think you've ever told me your last name, Beau."

"It's Beau Rather."

"How long have you been working for Noah?"

He twirled her in a circle before responding. "Just from the beginning of the year."

"Where were you working before that?"

Beau tugged her closer into his arms. "Oh, here and there. A cowpoke goes wherever the job is, although one day soon I hope to settle down with a spread of my own."

Did she dare ask him where he planned to start a ranch?

The music came to an end. She stepped back, but Beau

kept hold of her hand.

"How about we get something to drink?"

She nodded. "We could get a glass and take it over to my family. I'd love for you to meet them."

"There will be time for that later."

Kitty frowned, glancing toward where her sisters stood with their husbands, wishing they'd come to her rescue. Somehow being with Beau wasn't as exciting as she'd thought it would be. Maybe it was because she still held some hurt about how he'd immediately assumed she'd compromised her morals when she'd been with Noah. *Oh, Lord. What's wrong with me? Help me to forgive Beau... and Noah.*

Beau pressed a glass of cider into her hand. "Let's take a quick swig and get back on the dance floor again. I don't plan to waste any time." He winked at her.

Kitty took a small sip of the tart apple beverage. She couldn't help shooting a glance at Noah. Had he danced with anyone yet? Would he ask her?

She shoved the thought down. *Stop being so fickle. You already have a man interested in you.*

"Are you ready?" Beau took the mostly full glass from her hands before she could protest. He set it on a table before leading her to the dance floor again.

A lively jig started, leaving little opportunity to converse as they went through the movements of the dance. Kitty welcomed the respite, although she couldn't help wondering why it felt awkward talking with Beau in the church when he often made a point of speaking to her at the ranch.

The music continued to swirl around the room as couples moved in a fast pace. Kitty could barely catch her breath as they swayed one way and then another. While she'd always enjoyed the annual dance, she couldn't help peering toward the side of the room, at those standing along the wall. Or at least someone standing with his arms folded tight against his chest, a frown marring his face. What could possibly have riled Noah so much?

"So, are you going to keep glaring at Beau and Kitty, or are you going to head over there and ask her for a dance?"

Noah turned the glare on his foreman. "Maybe you should stay out of it. Your interfering last week did little good."

Henry's brow rose. "What're you talking about?"

Heat flared on Noah's neck. He'd never let Kitty or Henry know that he'd overheard their conversation in the kitchen.

His foreman's eyes twinkled.

No doubt the man had known Noah stood in the hallway.

"She keeps looking over here. The least you can do is go rescue her." Henry bumped against Noah's shoulder with his own.

"What makes you think she needs rescuing?" If anything, she looked perfectly content in Beau's arms.

"Because I happen to know a few things about women. Or at least one."

Henry's words caused Noah to swing his gaze to his

friend. "What're you talking about?"

His foreman fiddled with the Stetson in his hands for a minute before releasing a sigh. "I was married a long time ago."

Noah wrinkled his forehead. He'd heard nothing about Henry having a wife before.

Henry's voice softened. "She was the best thing to ever happen to me other than my relationship with the Almighty."

"What happened?"

He hefted a deep sigh. "She got pregnant right away. We couldn't be happier as we planned for the little one." Henry stared at the dancers for a few minutes, not saying anything else.

Noah let the silence lapse between them, knowing his foreman would share more when he was ready.

The dance ended and another started. Beau continued to keep Kitty in his arms on the floor.

He turned away from the sight, instead focusing on the man who'd been in his life since he could remember. Noah laid a hand on the man's shoulder as Henry's Adam's apple bobbed in his throat.

"My Melody went into labor. We didn't live close to town or a doctor. She had trouble with the birth pains right from the start... We both knew something wasn't right but didn't know what to do."

Noah stayed quiet, waiting for Henry to continue again.

"She didn't make it." He sniffed, tugging a handkerchief from his pocket and wiping his nose. "The baby either. I buried them that day, packed my things, and left Illinois.

Never been back since. Signed on with your pa just before you were born."

"I'm sorry, Henry." He tightened his grip on his friend's shoulder.

His foreman shoved the handkerchief back into his pants. "I only tell you now so you realize you shouldn't waste time. Get out there and ask her for a dance."

"But obviously, she's enjoying her time with Beau. It's their third one together."

Henry's eyes twinkled. "*Obviously*, you've been keeping count. Now go rescue the gal."

"Do you really think she wants me to?" Noah couldn't help studying the couple.

Just then, Kitty's gaze sought his again. She smiled at him.

It was all the invitation he needed.

He shoved away from the wall, nearly stumbling over his feet in his haste to get to her.

Her smile broadened as he grew closer.

He tapped Beau on the shoulder. "I believe it's my turn to dance with the little lady."

His ranch hand frowned at him. "I know you're in charge at the ranch, but you aren't here. Besides, Kitty's enjoying being with me." He shortened the gap between his and Kitty's frame.

She took a step backward, tugging her hand free from the cowboy, placing it in Noah's.

Noah startled when Henry came to stand beside him.

Folks were starting to chatter at the scene unfolding on the dance floor.

"I think it's time you found another partner for a bit."

Henry patted Beau between the shoulders, urging him to move away.

A scowl crossed the man's face, but he finally conceded and stalked off the floor.

Henry bowed to Kitty, grasping her other hand and kissing it. "I believe the two of you are long overdue for a spin around the floor together." He winked and strolled away.

A rosy blush swelled on Kitty's cheeks as Noah gathered her into his arms.

His heart stampeded as they swayed together. If only she knew how much he cared about her. But how could he convey it in a way that she'd actually believe him?

"Thank you." Her words were soft.

"For what?"

"I've been hoping you'd ask me to dance." Her blue eyes shone.

"You have?" He caught himself from nearly tripping over her feet.

She nodded.

Silence stretched for a few seconds until she caught his gaze again.

"I've been meaning to… that is…" She took a deep breath, slowly releasing it. "I wanted to let you know I forgive you."

His heart swelled at her words. Did it mean one day he'd have a chance with her?

"Henry said little boys often act differently than little girls." She licked her lips.

"I'm sorry for how poorly I treated you when we were in school. It was wrong of me. I should've known that little girls should be regarded differently than fellas. It's something I've regretted for a long time now." *Longer than she'll ever know. I never meant for you to think I didn't care about you.* If only he could tell her that to her face.

She rested a hand on his chest.

His heart immediately started pattering out of control.

"I forgive you, Noah. Henry thought..." Her face grew even rosier than before. She dipped her head so he couldn't see her eyes. "Never mind about that. I wanted you to know all the past is forgiven. Let's not bring it up again."

Her smile was nearly his undoing.

"I'd appreciate it, Kitty." Was now the time to say more about his feelings for her?

He drew her a little closer, relishing having her in his arms. Something he often dreamed about. *Is now the time, Lord?*

"I hope we can always be good friends." Her words yanked him from his prayer.

Friends? I want much more than to be her friend, Lord.

Chapter Eight

K itty had no sooner finished the dance with Noah when another man bowed before her.

"I'd be delighted if you would do me the pleasure of dancing with me." The blonde-haired man smiled at her as he motioned toward the general store clerk. "I believe you know my grandfather, Thomas Warren. I'm his eldest grandson, Winston."

Noah still lingered at Kitty's side. He thrust out his right hand toward the stranger. "Welcome to the area, Winston. I'm Noah Eldridge."

The two men shook hands before Mr. Warren turned back to Kitty, his eyebrows quirked.

"Welcome, Mr. Warren. I'd love to dance with you." She accepted his arm as he led her to the dance floor. "Your grandpa mentioned you'd be arriving soon. So, what are your thoughts of Yoder Grove so far?"

"It's a big change from the bustle of Kansas City, but I'm beginning to understand why Grandfather loves it so much."

Kitty glanced at his light-blue eyes.

His gaze jerked to the floor.

Odd. Was he just shy, or had his grandpa persuaded his grandson to dance with her?

She scanned the room. Beau stood with arms crossed, glaring at her. Kitty shifted her attention away from him only to find Noah watching her as well. Was it her imagination, or did he look as if he'd lost his best friend? Had something happened in the last few minutes that she wasn't aware of?

"Grandfather says you're a wonderful cook." His words stirred Kitty's attention back to her dancing partner.

She tilted her head and studied his face again. A muscle in his jaw twitched. "Some folks say so. It's something I really enjoy doing."

"I've heard you're working at a local ranch?"

Kitty nodded. "For now, until Noah can find someone." Come to think of it, when was the last time he heard about potential prospects? He hadn't mentioned anything to her recently. Her heart constricted at the thought of not seeing the ranch hands every day. They had a way of making her laugh, as well as heaping praise on her with each meal she created.

"I don't suppose you have time to take pity on a couple of bachelors and make a few meals for us too, would you?" Mr. Warren's cheeks filled with color. "I've never been able to cook worth anything. Turns out Grandfather isn't much better. Most times he eats items from his stock on the store shelves."

Was that what his dance invitation was all about? Trying to get her to cook for them? Kitty shook her head. Since when did she get so pessimistic? "Perhaps I can find the time to make a meal or two for you."

A grin spread across the young man's face. "That would be greatly appreciated."

Kitty worked to soothe her ruffled thoughts as she would smooth the disheveled fur of a dog. She didn't understand why she was so out of sorts.

The music came to an end. Kitty stepped back, clapping with the rest of the dancers.

"I'd better go check on my grandfather." Mr. Warren bowed, leaving her in the middle of the floor.

Her mouth gaped open for a second, and she shook her head. Kitty made her way to her sisters and their spouses.

Essie yawned as she rocked Miriam in her arms. "We're about ready to head home. With getting up in the middle of the night for feedings, I tire quickly. Are you ready to leave yet, or will one of your many suitors be bringing you home?"

Teddy hiked a brow, but didn't say anything.

"I suppose I'm ready too."

"Who's the new fella?" Teddy fell into step with her as they strolled toward the vestibule to collect their coats.

"Which one?" Essie bumped into Kitty's shoulder. "You had several tonight."

Heat sprang up her neck. "The first one was Beau Rather. He's one of Noah's men. The last man I danced with is Mr. Winston Warren."

"Is he related to the general store owner?" Jud took the

baby from Essie while helping her with her coat.

"His grandson." Kitty shoved her arm through the sleeve of her own jacket.

"So now you've got three fellas clammerin' for your attention." Teddy's eyes glinted.

"Three? There were only two that I danced with that you didn't know."

"Wasn't talkin' about new ones, but of the lot of them, you seemed the chummiest with Noah Eldridge. Never thought I'd see the day when you were cozyin' up to the fella who gave you the most grief through the years." She threw back her head, laughing. "If I didn't know any better, from the look on your face when you were dancin' with Noah, I'd think you'd finally found someone to settle down with." Teddy waggled her eyebrows before she took Paul's arm and stepped outside.

Kitty's heart stuttered. She had to admit that of the three men, she'd enjoyed her time the most with Noah. Probably only because they had finally settled the discomfort between them, and they had known each other the longest amount of time. It wasn't as though she had any intention of falling in love with the man. Teddy couldn't have it more wrong. Besides, what did her youngest sister know of love? Both Essie and Kitty had to tell their youngest sister about her care of their neighbor, Paul Baker.

Come to think of it. Teddy and Kitty had to make Essie aware of her affection for Jud when he'd shown up on their doorstep wounded, and their oldest sister had nursed him back to health.

There was no way Kitty wouldn't recognize love when

it came knocking at her door. One thing she was assured of—it certainly wouldn't involve Noah Eldridge.

"Hello, darling."

Noah cringed as he watched Beau greet Kitty as she arrived at the ranch the next morning, helping her down from her mare.

"Rather!" He couldn't help bellowing the hand's name.

Beau kissed Kitty's hand before shifting his gaze to Noah. "What is it?" A scowl darkened the man's face.

"Did you finish mucking the stalls?"

"Not yet. I'll get to it in a bit. Had to speak to my gal first."

"How about you get to it now instead of jawing with the help?" As soon as the words flew from Noah's mouth, he wished he could retrieve them, especially when a look of hurt flashed across Kitty's face.

"I'll have to talk with you later, Beau. Apparently, the *help* needs to get to work too." She lifted her skirt a smidgen, stomping up the steps to the house.

Beau's eyes darkened before he stalked off to the barn.

"That went over well." Henry leaned against the wooden fence lining the side yard.

"I don't want to hear it right now." He trudged to the water trough, tempted to dunk his head in it. Instead, he dipped his hand into the water, dribbling it onto his hot neck. Maybe it would help to cool his simmering emotions.

"They say you'll attract more flies with honey." Henry's

brow needled upward.

"Well, then it's a good thing I don't plan on attracting any." He turned on his heel, hoping his foreman would take the hint.

The man fell into step beside Noah. "You want to talk about it?"

His friend sounded like a woman... trying to get Noah to spill his feelings. Wasn't it enough that Kitty now had two other men interested in her? He'd never be able to compete with them. Might as well admit it, there wasn't any way he'd be able to persuade Kitty to consider him.

Kitty slammed the lid onto the kettle of boiling potatoes. *Who does that man think he is, calling me the help? I agreed to come and feed his men only because it's something Mama would've done. And what thanks have I gotten for all my labor? He treats me as if I'm a common employee.*

The sound of chuckling snagged her from her tirade.

"You two are like twin peas." Henry shook his head as he came into the room. "Neither of you are willing to admit or see how much you care for each other. He's afraid to say something, and you can't see what's right in front of you. Sometimes I think love is wasted on the youth."

What was the foreman blathering on about?

Kitty shook her head. "I don't know where you got the thought Noah and I are..." Heat pumped into her face.

"Just stating what all the other men can see. Except for

Beau, that is." Henry pulled out a chair, collapsing into it. "If you ask me, I think the fella sweet-talks whatever young lady he comes across. Can't imagine he's the type to settle down anytime soon."

Had she somehow misread Beau's intentions?

"Talked to him the other day." Henry rubbed his jaw. "Sounds like the man hasn't stayed on a job for more than a few months at a time."

Surely, he planned to stay in the area. Beau wouldn't be sparking her if he didn't, would he? He'd mentioned wanting to have a spread of his own. Had that been Beau's way of stating his interest in her?

Kitty grabbed a towel, wrapping it around the handle of the pot as she drained the water from the potatoes into a bowl to dump outside later. She tipped the steaming spuds onto a cutting board to cool before slicing them.

Henry continued to watch her as she worked.

A sound at the back door caused them both to look in that direction.

Beau smiled as he carried a basket. "I gathered the eggs for you, Kitty, with the hope you'd make some for breakfast."

"Does that mean all the mucking is finished?" Henry stood, taking the basket from the ranch hand.

Kitty watched as Beau clenched his jaw.

"Thanks, Beau. I appreciate it." She stared back and forth between the two men. There was some type of communication going on between them she didn't understand.

"You'd best get back to your chores." Henry's voice

dropped a notch, almost coming across as a menacing sound.

She hurried forward, placing a hand on Beau's arm. "Before you go, I had a question for you." She cast a tentative glance at the foreman.

He gave a brief nod but didn't leave the room.

Kitty swallowed, trying to push past the sudden lump lining her throat. "You, uh, mentioned wanting to purchase a spread sometime soon." Heat shimmied up her neck. "Do you have a place in mind around here?"

"Oh, I don't plan to live in Kansas." He winked at her. "It's too cold. I plan to head back to Texas soon. Hopefully, you'll be going with me."

Noah was just about ready to kick Beau out of the kitchen when he heard the man's words to Kitty. He didn't wait around to hear her response. His stomach rumbled as he strutted to the barn.

"Is it time for breakfast yet, boss?" Shorty stepped out of one of the stalls, a pitchfork filled with manure.

Noah bit back a growl. "I thought Rather was on the rotation for mucking today." The muscles in his neck knotted. Everywhere he went, there was a reminder of the man.

Shorty's head dipped. "I was here, so figured to do it."

He wouldn't be surprised if Beau hadn't enlisted Shorty's help so Beau could court Kitty instead of doing the work

Noah had instructed.

"Boss?" Shorty's brow puckered.

"I imagine it'll be ready sometime soon."

"Can I do something for you?"

Noah shook his head. "Just going to head into town. Don't know when I'll be back." He didn't wait for Shorty to respond. He traipsed down toward the end stall, throwing a saddle onto his stallion. A few minutes later, he rode off toward town.

He made it only a few miles down the road before he caught up with Paul Baker. Noah waved to him.

"Howdy, Noah. Where are you heading so early in the morning?"

Even though the man was a little younger than Noah, Paul had been one of the ones he'd played with when they were in school.

Reining his horse, he shrugged. He didn't have a destination in mind. No place in town would be open this early. "Nowhere in particular."

Paul studied him, not saying anything.

Noah forced himself not to squirm under the man's perusal.

"Why don't you come to the house for a visit? It's been a while since we jawed together." Paul grinned at him. "Teddy's cooking isn't nearly as good as Kitty's, but she's improving. You're welcome to eat breakfast with us. I'm on my way home from delivering some eggs in town. Teddy would've gone, but she's been sleeping in the past couple mornings."

What could it hurt? Henry would see that the men

checked on the herd. Noah would apologize later for how he'd treated his foreman. "Are you sure it won't be an imposition if Teddy isn't feeling well?"

"I don't think she's sick, just not as lively as normal." Paul shot him a look. "But don't go telling her I told you that."

Noah chuckled. Maybe some time away from the ranch would do him good.

The men fell into a comfortable silence as their horses trotted toward the Baker farm. They'd no sooner swung down from their saddles when Teddy came out onto the porch.

"I see you brought a visitor." She peered at Noah for a second before flipping her long braid over her shoulder. "Food's about ready." She turned her back and headed into the house again.

Paul shrugged as they climbed the steps. "Can't always cipher what a gal is thinking." He threw his head back, laughing. "In fact, it's pretty rare."

So maybe Noah wasn't the only one who struggled with a Love sister. Although he didn't know how much help Paul would be. At least *he'd* figured out how to marry one of them.

CHAPTER NINE

K itty kept watching the doorway to the dining room, but Noah still hadn't appeared for breakfast. Could he have taken ill? All the other men had recovered from their bouts of sickness, but maybe Noah wasn't feeling well. She nibbled on her lip, contemplating whether to check on him.

Henry rested a hand momentarily on her shoulder. "I'm sure he's fine." His words were said in a low voice.

She'd been out of sorts since Noah's comment earlier as well as Beau's proclamation of having no desire to live in Kansas. She shot a glance in his direction.

He winked at her before shoving some eggs into his mouth.

"Sure hope you can stay on permanent-like, Miss Love." Shorty rubbed his belly. "I don't think we've ever eaten so good."

The rest of the cowboys nodded.

That had never been part of Kitty's plan. Noah's either, but she couldn't help wishing it could be. It brought joy to her heart to fix food for the men each day. They always made a point of paying her compliments. She'd regret the loss of a job, if it ever happened... and them.

Her gaze found the empty chair at the head of the table again. She'd miss Noah too. Tears pricked Kitty's eyes as she studied each of the cowboys.

The thought surprised her. When had they gone from enemies to... friends? Even with his hurtful comment earlier, she couldn't help being concerned about why he'd missed the meal.

"Well, fellas, you know the assignments for the day. Best get at it."

Henry's words stirred Kitty from her thoughts. All the men shoved in their chairs, thanking her for the meal before carrying their dishes to the kitchen. Ever since her first day at the ranch, they'd made a point of doing what they could to make things easier for her. Probably didn't want to do anything to cause her not to come and cook for them.

"Something on your mind?"

Apparently, Kitty had lapsed into her musings again. "Can we somehow check on Noah?"

"Not sure where to look for him." Henry held her chair for her as she stood.

"What do you mean? He isn't on the ranch?" Her hand trembled as she picked up her plate.

"Here. Allow me." Henry stacked her plate and utensils on top of his, the cutlery clattering against the dishes. "Shorty mentioned Noah was heading to town, although I suspect he just wanted to get away for a bit."

She led the way to the kitchen. "Why do you think he left?"

The foreman stacked the dishes on the small table. He turned to face her, his brow arched. "I suspect it has something to do with Beau."

Kitty dipped her head as she shaved flakes from the soap bar before pouring hot water into the large dishpan. What did Beau have to do with Noah other than being his boss?

"I best see to the men." Henry tugged his Stetson from a hook by the back door. "Ring the dinner bell if you need anything."

She opened her mouth to question him on the matter, but he was already pulling the door closed behind him.

A sigh escaped her lips. "Looks like I need to figure out on my own why Noah was so bothered by Beau."

But after washing the stacks of dishes and pans, Kitty had gotten no closer to solving the conundrum of Noah Eldridge. With only having the experience of sisters, she didn't know if she'd ever be able to figure how a man thought.

The conversation and visit with Paul and Teddy Baker had gone better than Noah had expected. Especially because it gave him clarity about how to proceed with his problems. At least one of them. It was about time he had an open and honest conversation with Kitty, providing he could make sure Beau was occupied elsewhere and didn't interrupt them.

He reined his horse to a halt and swung down from the saddle.

Henry rode toward him. "It's about time you showed up." His lips twitched beneath his mustache. "That little gal in there's been worried something fierce."

Noah couldn't resist a smile from spreading. Maybe his conversation with Kitty would finally go over well. "I'm sorry for not responding better earlier."

Henry grinned. "You've had other things on your mind. Speaking of which…" He glanced to where the men were working in the far pasture. "I think it's about time we let Beau go."

He shook his head. "When I wanted to, you told me no. What's changed?"

The foreman swung down from the saddle, wrapping the reins around the hitching post. "He's been uncooperative all morning and downright refuses to do his assigned chores. We don't need that kind of weed infesting and stirring the men to thinking Beau's kind of behavior won't be addressed with stern consequences. Besides, I think we have more than enough men for the winter. I know your pa liked to hire most all the fellas who showed up looking for work, and you've followed in his footsteps. But I think this is one time when you need to make an exception."

Releasing Beau might help Noah's prospects with Kitty, but it could bring some backlash too. Maybe it would be best to delay the conversation with Beau until Noah first had the conversation with Kitty. "I'll keep it under advisement."

"Now, I'm wondering too...are you sure you're feeling alright?" He rested his hand on Noah's shoulder. "A while back you couldn't wait to get rid of the man. What's changed?"

He squirmed under the older man's perusal. "Can I get back to you on that?"

Henry's brows arched high on his forehead.

"I need to make things right with Kitty first."

"And hopefully finally say things plainly so she has no doubt of your feelings for her?" A twinkle shone in Henry's eyes. "I've been trying to do my own preparing for you."

What exactly did that mean? Noah hated to think what had transpired while he'd been away. He wouldn't put it past his foreman coming outright and telling Kitty how he'd pined for her for years. *I best get in there.* "I'll catch up with you later." He didn't wait for his friend to respond, vaulting the steps to the house.

He forced his erratic breathing under control before entering the kitchen.

The sound of his boots must've alerted Kitty to his presence because her head came up as he crossed the threshold.

"There you are." She rushed over, grabbing hold of his arm. "Are you hurt? Did something happen? I hope you didn't catch the ague, although it's been a little while since the other men were sick." Kitty flicked moisture from her eyes. "I've been worried and afraid I did something to upset you."

Noah cleared his throat. "I'm the one who needs to apologize to you."

Her brow wrinkled.

"Why don't we sit down for a few minutes?" He motioned to the table.

"Alright." She removed her hand from his arm.

He missed the warmth of it as soon as she did. They crossed the small room, and he tugged out a chair for her, waiting for her to be seated. He sank into a seat across from her. How Noah longed to take her hands in his, but he hadn't earned that right yet. Hopefully, he would someday. *Keep on track, Eldridge.*

Kitty's hands fidgeted in her lap.

"I should've never spoken about you the way I did this morning." He started to shove his hands through his hair when he realized he still wore his Stetson. Heat surged to his face as he removed it, setting the hat on the seat beside him.

She bit her lip before speaking. "Why did you say it?"

Because I've been a jealous fool, that's why. He exhaled a sigh. "It had nothing to do with you."

"Then what bothered you? I guess it *is* true that I'm only the help." She ducked her head again.

Noah curled his finger under her chin, lifting her head. "I've never thought of you like that. You willingly came to help a... friend in need. I can't ever thank you enough for how you responded to my needs... er... the men too." His gaze dropped to her lips before he forced himself to stay on task.

Her cheeks turned a becoming rosy color as her eyes widened.

He let his hand fall away, afraid of scaring her off. Noah

still needed to learn where he stood with her compared to Beau.

"Then why did you mention my being the help?"

This wasn't going at all the way he'd hoped. He had a knack for getting tongue-tied when she looked at him like that.

The back door opened, and Shorty stepped inside. "Did you want me to take care of your horse, boss? Saw him at the hitching post."

Honestly, Lord? You aren't making this easy for me.

"I appreciate it, Shorty, but I plan to join you fellas soon."

The man nodded. "Did you happen to pick up some more coffee when you were in town? Our supply in the bunkhouse is getting low."

"I didn't make it to town after all." He forced himself not to respond to his cowhand in frustration. Noah had done enough of that recently. "Was there anything else?"

"Did you want me to start a list of other supplies we need?"

"Sure. Maybe one of you can go into town later to get them. Miss Love might have a list too." He glanced at her, and she nodded.

"You've got it, boss." Shorty dipped his hat and closed the door behind him.

He'd no sooner left when Beau strolled into the room.

Noah curled his fingers beneath the table trying to tamper his frustration. *I thought You gave me the go-ahead for talking to Kitty, Lord. Did I misunderstand?*

A smug expression crossed Beau's face as he winked at Kitty. "Just checking in to see how you're doing, darling."

Her gaze darted between the man and Noah. "Fine, although I think it's best if you returned to your work. I need to as well, or lunch won't be ready in time." She pushed back her chair and stood.

Noah couldn't keep the sternness from his voice as he also stood. "Beau, get back on the job."

The ranch hand had the audacity to raise his eyebrows, almost daring Noah to do something about it.

Kitty's gaze crashed into his before swinging toward Beau. "It's best if you leave and do what Noah says."

"I'll do it for *you*, darling." He glowered at Noah, turned on his heel, and left.

"I'm sorry about that." Kitty picked up a rag and wiped the table.

"Wasn't your fault." He forced himself to calm and spit out what needed to be said before anyone else interrupted them. "Now, back to your question, Kitty. I wasn't frustrated with you this morning, but with Beau. Either way, though, it's no excuse for treating you so poorly. I shouldn't have acted the way I did. Will you please forgive me?"

She gave a brief nod. "Why does Beau bother you so much?" Her gaze darted to his before dropping.

He squirmed. Would she believe him if he told her he'd been jealous of his ranch hand? A muscle twitched in Noah's jaw as silence stretched between them. *Lord, help me use the right words here.* He took a deep breath. It was now or never. "I admit it's been painful watching Beau fawn all over you when I lo—"

A rap thudded against the back kitchen door.

He bit back a groan. "Now who can that be?" Noah crossed

the room, throwing the door open. Just when he'd finally gotten enough courage to tell Kitty how he really felt about her.

"Are you Noah Eldridge?" A tall man stood with a Stetson in his hand, his fingers curling around the brim. "Saw your advertisement for a cookie, and I'm here to apply for the job."

Really, Lord? You chose now to send someone to take Kitty's place? What were You thinking?

CHAPTER TEN

Kitty slipped away from the ranch as soon as she'd
heard Noah agree to the stranger's offer of staying on
as a cook for Noah's men. She hadn't taken the time to say
farewell to any of them. Her heart broke as she urged her
horse to a faster pace.

Tears trailed down her cheeks. Kitty wiped them with the
back of her glove. *What am I going to do now, Lord? So much
for thinking I'd finally found my place.* Her heart felt like a steer
sat on it. She could barely catch her breath.

As she turned onto the path toward the house, Kitty
halted her mount. *I can't go home just yet.* Decision made,
she changed directions, heading to Teddy and Paul's place.
Even though there was an equal number of years between
both her older and younger sisters, Kitty had found
talking to Teddy somehow easier through the years. Maybe
because she had exceptional insight and wasn't afraid to
state the truth.

Minutes later, Kitty slipped from her horse, knocking on

the door to her sister's home.

It creaked open. A smudge of flour dotted Teddy's cheek. "Figured you'd be comin' soon, just didn't know when to expect you."

"Why would you think I'd be visiting anytime soon?" Kitty closed the door behind her. Stripping off her gloves, she strolled to the fireplace, extending her hands toward the roaring fire.

"Thought after Noah finally got around to sharin' his love, you'd want to talk it over." Teddy picked up a rolling pin, running it back and forth over a slab of dough on the floured table surface.

"Wait! What?" Surely Kitty had misheard her sister.

Teddy smacked her forehead with her floured hand, creating another white mark on her face. "Did I go and ruin it? Thought for sure he planned to tell you first-thing."

"What are you talking about? Noah doesn't love me. Besides, you've always told me to avoid the man." She crossed to the table, sinking into a chair. "And how would you know about any of it?"

"So, he hadn't spoken with you yet?" Teddy went back to her rolling.

"Sort of, but we got interrupted." She scrunched her eyes, trying to remember the last words Noah had spoken before the new cook had shown up at the back door. *Think. Think.*

His final words came to her in a flash. Something about finding it difficult to watch Beau's interaction with her. But there was something else too... *when I lo—* Was Noah going to say love? Her heart skipped a beat, unsure of how she felt about the idea.

She shook her head, trying to clear her muddled thoughts. "You still haven't shared how you're aware of this."

Teddy didn't answer right away. She set the rolling pin aside, dusting flour on the bottom of a pie tin before draping the crust over the top of it. Wiping her hands on an apron, she settled in a chair across from Kitty. "He stopped by here earlier."

Her pulse skittered. "What did he say?"

"Turns out we've been wrong about the man. I should know by now that fellas think differently on account of being married to one. Act different too. From what Noah said, he's been smitten with you ever since he was a young fella. Just never knew how to tell you."

"He did? He does?"

"Except he's afraid you've got your heart set on that scoundrel Beau." Her brows crashed over her eyes. "I can tell you outright, he didn't give me a good impression at the dance. Paul, Essie, and Jud felt the same way too. Anyone who doesn't introduce himself to family members can't be trusted, if you ask me."

"I'm not interested in him. Turns out he doesn't plan to stay in Kansas." Kitty twisted her hands in her lap. "I don't think I could ever live far away from all of you. Ever since being a little girl, I dreamed of all of us settling down around here and raising families together."

"It does say in the Bible about leavin' and cleavin'." Teddy reached for Kitty's hands. "But it sure would be nice if we all lived nearby."

"Are you saying I should consider Beau?"

Teddy wagged her head from side to side vigorously.

"Not at all. Somethin' didn't sit right when I saw the fella. Paul thinks he's a smooth talker."

"I think at first, it flattered me having a man interested. But the more I've gotten to know Beau..." Kitty shrugged.

"Have you been praying about it?"

Teddy's words pricked. To be honest, she hadn't been doing a lot of praying on the matter.

Her sister released her hands. "I'm guessin' that's a no. If you ask me, you've been in love with Noah all along, or you wouldn't have agreed to help him."

Teddy couldn't be right, could she?

Heat flushed her face as Kitty remembered when Noah had been intently looking at her lips. Had he wanted to kiss her? Would she want him to? She blinked away sudden tears. "None of it matters since I won't be seeing him anymore."

"Why not?"

"Because I've lost my job." She sniffed. "Noah found a cook, so there won't be any reason for me to return to the ranch."

"How's that make you feel?"

Kitty never thought she'd see the day where Teddy spoke about feelings. "It's killing me." She couldn't hold back a sob.

Her sister came around the table, sinking into a chair beside Kitty, pulling her into her arms. "Go ahead and cry it out. You'll feel better."

She sobbed as her heart broke. Tears continued to flow until only hiccupping sighs were left. Kitty sat back, wiping her cheeks on the handkerchief Teddy had provided.

"I think it's time to face the thought that you love Noah Eldridge."

Deep in her heart, she knew Teddy had recognized Kitty's feelings before she had. She sniffed again, balling the handkerchief in her hand. "What am I going to do about it? It's not like I can just go over there and declare my love for him."

"Why not?"

Noah had to find Kitty. He thought for sure she'd be at home, but her brother-in-law, Jud, told Noah she'd left early and hadn't returned. Jud suggested checking with Teddy and Paul Baker. Noah turned his stallion toward their home. *Please let her be there, Lord. I need to see her.* He'd been frustrated to have their conversation interrupted, and for a new cook to show up unexpectedly, even though he'd advertised for one.

The time seemed to drag before he came upon the Baker homestead. Noah breathed a sigh of relief when he spotted Kitty's mare tied to the hitching post in the front of the house. *Thank You, Lord.* He swung from the saddle, walked toward the porch, and clomped up the steps. It took everything in him to refrain from pounding on the door.

It screeched open.

Teddy grinned and winked at him. "Knew you'd be here soon." She motioned him inside.

Kitty stood as soon as she caught sight of him. "Noah?"

"I've been looking everywhere for you." He hurried over to her, stopping only inches away. He refrained from drawing her into his arms. "Would you mind if we stepped outside so we can talk?"

She shrugged into her coat and followed him.

They strolled away from the house. Turning, he reached for her hand. "I didn't mean for you to rush off before we could finish our discussion."

Her eyelashes fluttered as she studied him.

At least she hadn't pulled back when he took her hand in his. He hoped it was a good sign.

Taking a deep breath, Noah gathered his courage. "I've been trying to tell you for weeks that I love you. Have for many years, in fact. Think I even did as a child, which is why I liked teasing you so much. I'm sorry for hurting you. It was never my intention. Truth is, I can't imagine my life without you."

"Truly?" Her lips curled in a smile.

Noah cradled her face in his hand. "I know you may already have an understanding with Beau, but I hope you'll consider me."

She shook her head, her eyes sparkling.

"I understand." He took a step back, dropping his hand to his side.

Kitty giggled and grabbed his hand, placing it back on her face again. "I'm not interested in Beau."

His gaze darted to hers. "You're not?"

"I realize it's *you* I look forward to seeing and talking to each day." Her eyes sparkled. "When I learned you wouldn't need me anymore, it was heartbreaking."

"There won't ever be a day I don't need you, sweetheart." He leaned in as he glanced at her lips, seeking silent permission to kiss her.

She didn't hesitate, rising on tiptoe to meet his lips with hers.

His heart pattered as he deepened the kiss.

Kitty didn't know how much time passed as she stood kissing Noah in the middle of Teddy and Paul's front yard. Her cheeks flushed as she brought their sweet kisses to an end. Kitty's heart flipped with wild abandon. "I love you, Noah Eldridge."

He leaned his head against her forehead. "Those are the best words I've ever heard other than reading about God's love for me." Noah kissed her cheek. "Do you think you'd ever consider marrying a man like me?"

Her heart pattered before lunging forward in a gallop. "Most definitely. There's nothing else that would bring me such wondrous pleasure than being your wife." She squealed as she pulled Noah into her arms, squeezing him tight. "I can't believe God finally answered my prayers for a husband. He always knows what's best for us, even when we can't see it." Kitty giggled. "I won't end up being an old spinster after all."

"Not if I can help it." He leaned in again, claiming her lips.

The sound of footsteps caused them to dart apart.

Kitty couldn't resist running a finger along the lips that

Noah had soundly branded as his.

"That's enough kissing for now." Paul winked as he got closer.

"Now, Paul, let them be." Teddy stepped down from the porch.

Kitty's cheeks burned. Had her sister and brother-in-law been watching them?

"I hope there was a marriage proposal amid all that kissin'." Teddy waggled her eyebrows. "Don't want to end up performin' a shotgun weddin'."

"Teddy!" Kitty shot a look at her sister.

Her sister's eyes danced.

Noah tugged Kitty to his side. "She's agreed to marry me, although she hasn't said when yet."

"How about Easter Sunday? It will give me enough time to sew a special dress." Kitty exchanged a tender glance with Noah. "And for us to get to know each other a little more, since for most of my life I thought of you as an enemy. Lord knew, it couldn't be farther from the truth."

"I can't think of anything finer than having our wedding be on the day our Lord and Savior rose from the grave." He planted a kiss on her nose. "I'll be counting the days until you're mine."

"Me too." Kitty didn't hesitate in drawing Noah into her arms, rising on tiptoe, and kissing him. She prayed he'd always know how special he was to her.

EPILOGUE

April 1, 1877

N oah had a hard time paying attention as the Easter church service was coming to a close. His heart rejoiced at the reminder of what Jesus had done for him when He rose from the grave. But Noah had to admit that his mind kept leaping to what came afterward — marrying the woman he'd loved for most of his life.

"Folks, Noah Eldridge and Kitty Love will be getting married this morning, and they'd be thrilled for you to join them for the ceremony." The pastor announced from the pulpit. "We'll get started in just a minute."

Noah's heart pounded as he stood and started toward the front of the church.

Henry came to stand beside him, clapping him on the shoulder. "You finally got your gal."

He turned to look toward the back of the church. All his cowhands lined the second pew grinning at him. All except Beau, who Noah had fired on the day he proposed to Kitty.

The music swelled as he caught movement at the very back. He got on the tips of his toes, struggling to catch sight of his beloved.

There she is.

Her light blue dress fluttered as Kitty strolled up the aisle, a smile spread wide. Her face lit with love for him.

Thank You, Lord, for answering my prayers.

It had taken Noah a while to woo his cook, but it had been worth it. He couldn't wait to claim the last Love sister as his own.

Kitty couldn't keep her eyes off Noah as she hurried down the aisle to meet him at the front of the church. She tugged Jud's arm, trying to get him to increase his pace.

Chuckles filled the church, but she didn't care what others thought of her. All she wanted to do was to become Noah's wife.

Her heart filled as she reached the man of her dreams and prayers. *Thank You, Lord, for forgiving me my sins and showing me of my need to forgive Noah. I could never have predicted what you had in store for us. I couldn't be more thankful.*

"Dearly beloved, we've gathered here..."

The ceremony passed quickly as Kitty and Noah exchanged their vows.

"You may now kiss your bride."

Her pulse thrummed as Noah gathered her in his arms. As Kitty's lips found his, she couldn't help feeling like she'd finally found her home.

More From Jodie Wolfe
From the

Time to Come Home series:

Abigail Stewart, with the Civil War raging, is on the verge of losing everything. The man who is responsible for her brother's death comes to Shippensburg offering to help. How can she work with her enemy? What's to stop him from betraying her?

Wounded during the war, Daniel Thompson must find a way to make amends and fulfil his friend's dying request. Daniel's homecoming proves anything but easy as he seeks to find forgiveness from his family when they can't be found. The woman he tries to assist, doesn't want anything to do with him.

Can two wounded hearts find their way back home?

Hannah Moore escapes the overbearing grip of her relatives and forges her own way in Shippensburg, PA, far away from their clutches. Despite Hannah's sheer determination, she finds life on her own daunting as she loses job after job. Unsure where she fits in, Hannah wonders if she'll ever be good enough. She feels as if God has forsaken her and questions if she will ever find a place to belong. The last thing she needs is an ignorant shop keeper constantly questioning her abilities and standing in her way. Hannah will take almost any position available so as not to return to the place of her upbringing.

Luke Weiser has one goal in mind—finding a way to save his grandmother and restore her health. Only trouble is, she has other ideas about what is best for her. Gran longs to see Luke's return to faith in the Lord, but he blames God for his grandmother's sickness and the tragic events of his childhood. After the death of his mother, followed by his father's abandonment, Luke refuses to trust his heart to anyone, and certainly not a wife. When Hannah keeps popping up in the hardware shop where he works, Luke is forced to think twice about his convictions.

Can two bruised hearts follow their personal quests and discover healing in the process?

Be watching for

Sarah's Search

By Jodie Wolfe

Book 3 of
Time to Come Home

Available Spring 2026

Step back in time to the Cherokee Strip Land Run, Oklahoma Territory in:

In 1893, on the eve of the great race for land, Benjamin David prays for God to guide him to his 'Promised Land'. Finding property and preaching to the lost are his only ways of honoring his deceased fiancée, but he didn't count on Elmer (Elsie) Smith claiming the same plot and refusing to leave. Not only is she a burr in his side, but she is full of the homesteading know-how he sadly lacks.

Obtaining a claim in the Cherokee Strip Land Run is Elsie Smith's only hope for survival, but not just any plot will do. She has a specific one in mind. The plot's not only a way to honor her pa and his life, but also to provide a livelihood for herself. Elsie's willing to do whatever it takes to get that piece of property, and she's determined to keep it, but she wasn't planning on a kind, handsome preacher standing in her way.

Her bitterness is what protects her, and she has no intentions of allowing that preacher to lay claim to her land . . . or her heart.

Jodie Wolfe creates novels where hope and quirky meet. She is a member of American Christian Fiction Writers (ACFW), and Faith, Hope, & Love Christian Writers (FHLCW). She's been a semi-finalist and finalist in various writing contests. A former columnist for *Home School Enrichment* magazine, her articles can be found online at: Crosswalk, Christian Devotions. When not writing she enjoys spending time with her husband in Pennsylvania, reading, and walking. Learn more at www.jodiewolfe.com.

A complete list of my novels can be found at jodiewolfe.com.

Are you interested in knowing when my next book is available? You can sign up for my newsletter, become my friend on Goodreads, or follow me on BookBub, Facebook, and Pinterest.

Newsletter: jodiewolfe.com
Goodreads: Jodie Wolfe
Bookbub: Jodie Wolfe
Facebook: Jodie Wolfe – Author Page
Pinterest: JodieAWolfe

If you loved my book, please consider leaving a review online at retail sites such as Amazon, Barnes & Noble, Goodreads, Bookbub, etc. The more reviews a book has, the more likely other readers can find it. Please help to spread the word.